Metroland

Julian Barnes

ROBIN CLARK

Published by Robin Clark Limited 1981
A member of the Namara Group
27/29 Goodge Street, London W1P 1FD
First published by Jonathan Cape Limited 1980

Manufactured in the USA

After three years as a lexicographer on the O.E.D. *Supplement*, Julian Barnes read for the bar and then began work as a freelance journalist, writing for *The Times Literary Supplement*, *The Times Educational Supplement*, *New Statesman*, *Oxford Mail*, *Sunday Times* and *Observer*. He was contributing editor of the *New Review*, where he wrote the 'Greek Street' column under the pseudonym of Edward Pygge. He is Deputy Literary Editor of the *Sunday Times* and television critic of the *New Statesman*. *Metroland* is his first novel.

'*Metroland* is a delicious book, sharp and witty and observant' *The Listener*

To Laurien

Contents

PART ONE
Metroland (1963)

A noir, E blanc, I rouge, U vert, O bleu
Rimbaud

There is no rule against carrying binoculars in the National Gallery.

On this particular Wednesday afternoon in the summer of 1963, Toni had the notebook and I had the glasses. So far, it had been a productive visit. There had been the young nun in men's spectacles who smiled sentimentally at the Arnolfini Wedding, and then, after a few moments, frowned and made a disapproving cluck. There had been the anoraked girl hiker, so transfixed by the Crivelli altarpiece that we simply stood on either side of her and noted the subtlest parting of the lips, the faintest tautening of skin across the cheekbones and the brow ('Spot anything on the temple your side?' 'Zero' – so Toni wrote down *Temple twitch; LHS only*). And there had been the man in the chalk-stripe suit, hair precisely parted an inch above his right ear, who twitched and squirmed in front of a small Monet landscape. He puffed out his cheeks, leaned back slowly on his heels, and exhaled like a discreet balloon.

Then we came to one of our favourite rooms, and one of our most useful pictures: Van Dyck's equestrian portrait of Charles I. A middle-aged lady in a red mackintosh was sitting in front of it. Toni and I walked quietly to the padded bench at the other end of the room, and pretended interest in a tritely jocund Franz Hals. Then, while he shielded me, I moved forward a little and focussed the glasses on her. We were far enough away for me to be able to whisper notes to Toni quite safely; if she heard anything, she'd take it for the usual background murmur of admiration and assent.

The gallery was fairly empty that afternoon, and the woman was quite at ease with the portrait. I had time to impart a few speculative biographical details.

'Dorking? Bagshot? Forty-five, fifty. Shoppers' return. Married, two children, doesn't let him fug her any more. Surface happiness, deep discontent.'

That seemed to cover it. She was gazing up at the picture now like an icon-worshipper. Her eyes hosed it swiftly up and down, then settled, and began to move slowly over its surface. At times, her head would cock sideways and her neck thrust forward; her nostrils appeared to widen, as if she scented new correspondences in the painting; her hands moved on her thighs in little flutters. Gradually, her movements quietened down.

'Sort of religious peace,' I muttered to Toni. 'Well, quasi-religious, anyway; put that.'

I focussed on her hands again; they were now clasped together like an altar-boy's. Then I tilted the binoculars back up to her face. She had closed her eyes. I mentioned this.

'Seems to be recreating the beauty of what's in front of her; or savouring the after-image; can't tell.'

I kept the glasses on her for a full two minutes, while Toni, his biro raised, waited for my next comment.

There were two ways of reading it: either she was beyond the point of observable pleasure; or else she was asleep.

1 · *Orange Plus Red*

Cut privet still smells of sour apples, as it did when I was sixteen; but this is a rare, lingering exception. At that age, everything seemed more open to analogy, to metaphor, than it does now. There were more meanings, more interpretations, a greater variety of available truths. There was more symbolism. Things contained more.

Take my mother's coat, for example. She had made it herself, on a dressmaker's dummy which lived under the stairs and told you everything and nothing about the female body (see what I mean?). The coat was reversible, pillar-box red on one side, an expansive black and white check on the other; the lapels, being made of the inner material, provided what the pattern called 'a dash of contrast at the neck' and chimed with the large square patch pockets. It was, I now see, a highly skilful piece of needlework; then, it proved to me that my mother was a turncoat.

This evidence of duplicity was corroborated one year when the family went to the Channel Islands for a holiday. The size of the coat's pockets, it transpired, was exactly that of a flat-pack of 100 cigarettes; and my mother walked back through the customs with 400 contraband Senior Service. I felt, by association, guilt and excitement; but also, further down, a private sense of being right.

Yet there was even more to be extracted from this simple coat. Its colour, like its structure, had secrets. One evening, walking home from the station with my mother, I looked at her coat, which was turned to show its red side, and noticed that it had gone brown. I looked at my mother's lips and they were brown. If she had withdrawn her hands from her (now murkily) white gloves, her fingernails, I knew, would also be brown. A trite occurrence nowadays; but in the first months of orange sodium lighting it was wonderfully disturbing. Orange on red gives dark brown. Only in suburbia, I thought, could it happen.

At school the next morning I pulled Toni out of a pre-assembly kickaround and told him about it. He was the confidant with whom I shared all my hates and most of my enthusiasms.

'They even fug up the spectrum,' I told him, almost weary at yet another outrage.

'What the fug do you mean?'

There was no ambiguity about the 'they'. When I used it, it meant the unidentified legislators, moralists, social luminaries and parents of outer suburbia. When Toni used it, it meant their inner London equivalents. They were, we had no doubt, exactly the same sort of people.

'The colours. The street lamps. They fug up the colours after dark. Everything comes out brown, or orange. Makes you look like moonmen.'

We were very sensitive about colours at that time. It had all started one summer holiday, when I'd taken Baudelaire with me to read on the beach. If you look at the sky through a straw, he said, it looks a much richer shade of blue than if you look at a large patch of it. I communicated the discovery to Toni on a postcard. After that, we started worrying about colours; they were – you couldn't deny it – ultimates, purities of extra value to the godless. We didn't want bureaucrats fugging around with them. They'd already got at

' ... the language ... '

' ... the ethics ... '

' ... the sense of priorities ... '

but these you could, in the last analysis, ignore. You could go your own swaggering way. But if they got at the colours? We couldn't even count on being ourselves any more. Toni's swarthy, thick-lipped Middle-European features would be completely negrified by sodium. My own snub-nosed, indeterminately English face (still excitedly waiting for its great leap into adulthood) was more immediately secure; but doubtless 'they' would think up some satirical ploy for it.

As you can see, we worried about large things in those days. And why not? When else can you get to worry about them? You wouldn't have caught us fretting about our future careers, because we knew that by the time we were grown up, the state would be paying people like us simply to exist, simply to walk about like sandwich-men advertising the good life. But stuff like the purity of the language, the perfectibility of self, the function of art, plus a clutch of capitalised intangibles like Love, Truth, Authenticity ... well, that was different.

Our coruscating idealism expressed itself naturally in a public pose of raucous cynicism. Only a strongly purifying motive could explain how hard and how readily Toni and I pissed on other people. The mottoes we deemed appropriate to our cause were *écraser l'infâme* and *épater la bourgeoisie*. We admired Gautier's *gilet rouge*, Nerval's lobster; our Spanish Civil War was the *bataille d'Hernani*. We chanted in concert:

> *Le Belge est très civilisé;*
> *Il est voleur, il est rusé;*
> *Il est parfois syphilisé;*
> *Il est donc très civilisé.*

The final rhyme delighted us, and we used to work the blurred homophone into our stilted French conversation classes at every opportunity. First, you would set up some worthy fumbler with a gallingly contemptuous remark delivered in simple language; the fumbler would lurch into

'*Je ne suis pas,* er, *d'accord avec ce qui, ce que?*' (a frowning look at the master) 'Barbarowski *a,* um, *juste dit ...* '

then one of our sniggering cabal would jump in, before the master could rouse himself from his depression at how thick the fumbler was, with a

'Carrément, M'sieur, je crois pas que Phillips soit assez syphilisé pour bien comprendre ce que Barbarowski vient de proposer ... '

—and every time they let it go.

We were, you may have guessed, mostly doing French. We cared for its language because its sounds were plosive and precise; and we cared for its literature largely for its combativeness. French writers were always fighting one another—defending and purifying the language, ousting slang words, writing prescriptive dictionaries, getting arrested, being prosecuted for obscenity, being aggressively Parnassian, scrabbling for seats in the Académie, intriguing for literary prizes, getting exiled. The idea of the sophisticated tough attracted us greatly. Montherlant and Camus were both goal-keepers; a *Paris-Match* photo of Henri de going up for a high ball, which I had sellotaped inside my locker, was as venerated as Geoff Glass's signed portrait of June Ritchie in *A Kind of Loving*.

There didn't seem to be any sophisticated toughs in our English course. There certainly weren't any goalkeepers. Johnson was tough, but hardly swish enough for us: after all, he hadn't even got across the Channel until he was nearly dead. Blokes like Yeats, though, were the other way round: swish, but always fugging around with fairies and stuff. How would they both react if all the reds in the world turned to brown? One would hardly notice it had happened; the other would be blinded by the shock.

2 · Two Small Boys

Toni and I were strolling along Oxford Street, trying to look like *flâneurs*. This wasn't as easy as it might sound. For a start, you usually needed a *quai* or, at the very least, a *boulevard*; and, however much we might be able to imitate the aimlessness of the *flânerie* itself, we always felt that we hadn't quite mastered what happened at each end of the stroll. In Paris, you would be leaving behind some rumpled couch in a *chambre particulière*; over here, we had just left behind Tottenham Court Road Underground station and were heading for Bond Street.

'How about écrasing someone?' I suggested, twirling my umbrella.

'Not really up to it. I did Dewhurst yesterday.' Dewhurst was a prefect destined for the priesthood, whom Toni had, we agreed, totally crushed in the course of a vicious metaphysical discussion. 'But I might be up to an épat.'

'Sixpence?'

'Okay.'

We wandered along while Toni looked for subjects. Ice-cream vendors? Small fry, and hardly bourgeois enough. That policeman? Too dangerous. They came into the same category as pregnant women and nuns. Suddenly, Toni hoiked his head at me and started pulling off his school tie. I did the same, rolled it round four fingers, and pocketed it. Now we were just two unidentifiable boys in white shirts, grey trousers, and black jackets lightly specked with dandruff. I followed him across the road towards a new boutique (how we disapproved of these linguistic imports); in large yellow capitals it announced MAN SHOP. It was, we suspected, one of those new and dangerous places where they're into the changing-room after you, with rape in mind, before you can pull up your trousers. Toni looked round the assistants and picked out the most respectable-looking: ageing, greying, separate collar, a thick margin of cuff, even a tie-pin. Clearly a left-over from the previous ownership.

'Yes, sir, can I help you?'

Toni gazed past him at the open-fronted wooden drawers of Banlon socks.

'I'd like one man and two small boys, please.'

'I beg your pardon?' said tie-pin.

'One man and two small boys, please,' repeated Toni in a dogged-customer voice. The rules of the épat declared that you should neither giggle nor give ground. 'It doesn't matter about the size.'

'I don't understand, sir.' That *sir* was pretty cool in the circs, I thought. I mean, the guy must be about to crack, mustn't he?

'For God's sake,' said Toni quite brusquely, 'call yourself a Man Shop? I can see I shall have to go elsewhere.'

'I suggest you do, sir. And which school are you at?'

We beat it.

'Cool fugger,' I complained to Toni as we flâned on at top speed.

'Yeah. Think I épated him much?'

'Must have done, must have done.' I'd been really impressed, especially by the way Toni had picked the right assistant, not just the one nearest the door. 'Anyway, you get your tanner.'

'I'm not worried about *that*. I just want to know if I épated him.'

' 'Course you did. 'Course you did. Wouldn't have asked for our school otherwise. Anyway, did you notice that *sir*?'

Toni gave a squint-grin, his mouth sliding across as if loyal to his eyes.

'Yeah.'

It was that time of life when being sirred is of inestimable importance; a token coveted out of all proportion to its value. It was better than being allowed to use the front steps at school; better than not having to wear a cap; better than sitting on the sixth-form balcony during break; better, even, than carrying an umbrella. And that was saying something. I once carried my umbrella to school and back every day of a three-month summer term during which it never rained. The status, not the function, counted. Inside the school, you displayed it – fencing with your peers, pinning the shoes of smaller boys to the floor with a sharpened ferrule; but outside, it made a man of you. Even if you were scarcely five feet, your face a battlefield of acne shaded by vigorous adolescent fuzz; even if you walked lopsidedly, weighed down by a festering cricket-bag full of rotting rugger shirts and gangrenous boots; as long as you had your umbrella, there was always an outside chance you might collect a *sir* from someone, an outside chance of a bout of surging pleasure.

On Monday mornings Toni and I would ask each other the same questions.

'Ecras anyone?'

' 'Fraid not.'

'Epat?'

'Well, not exactly ... '

'Sirred?'

A teasing smile of assent would rescue the whole weekend.

We counted the number of times we were sirred; we remembered the best occasions and retailed them to each other in the tones of old roués recalling conquests; and, of course, we never forgot the first time.

My own first time, on which I still dwelt happily, occurred when I was measured for my first pair of longs. It was in a thin, corridor-like shop in Harrow, which was wall-papered with boxes of clothes; racks of camouflage windcheaters and corduroy trousers as stiff as cardboard turned it into an obstacle course. Whatever colour you wore when you went into the shop, you always came out in grey or bottle-green. They did sell brown as well – but nobody, my mother assured me, wore brown until they were retired. On this occasion, I was booked to come out in grey.

My mother, though timid in her family and social life, was always precise and authoritarian in shops. Some deep instinct told her that here was one hierarchy which would never be disturbed.

'A pair of trousers, Mr Foster, please,' she asked in an unfamiliarly confident voice. 'Grey. Long.'

'Certainly, madam,' Mr Foster greased. Then, looking at me, 'Long. Certainly, sir.'

I could have fainted; I could, at the very least, have grinned. Instead I just stood, helpless with happiness, while Mr Foster knelt at my feet and piled on the praise.

'Just measure you up, sir. Look straight ahead. Shoulders back. Legs apart, sir, please. That's right.'

From around his neck he slipped a tape measure, the end six inches of which were stiffened with a brass plate. Holding it at inch 5 (presumably to avoid arrest), he stabbed me sharply three times in the perineum.

'Hold still, sir,' he wheedled, largely for my mother's benefit, in case she should wonder why he was taking so long. But there was no chance of my moving. Fear for one's gonads, fear even of being bundled into a changing-cubicle and roughly raped, meant nothing beside being acknowledged as a man. Such was the disorienting pleasure that it never even occurred to me to whisper, as a sort of alarming comfort, the school cry of 'Ruined!'

3 · Rabbit, Human

'RooooOOOOOOOOOiiiiined ... '

It was the school cry, drawn out and modulated in the way we imagined hyenas to howl. Gilchrist did the screechiest, most fearing version; Leigh one with a breaking sob in the middle of the vowel howl; but everyone did it at least adequately. It voiced, however playfully, the virgin's obsessive fear of castration. You came out with it on all appropriate occasions: when a chair was knocked over, a foot trodden on, a pencil case lost. It even came into our parody way of starting fights: combatants advanced on each other, the left hand clamped like a cricket box over the groin, the right hand outstretched, palm upwards, fingers working in the air like claws; meanwhile, onlookers let out miniature proxy squeaks of 'RoooOOined'.

But the parody had a chill to it. We had all read about Nazi castration by X-ray, and taunted one another with the possibility. If that happened, you were finished: literature proved that you got fat and ended up with a walk-on part, your only function being to make other people feel good. Either that, or economic circumstances forced you to become an opera singer in Italy. Quite how the whole terrifying process began, we were not altogether sure: but it had something to do with changing rooms, and public lavatories, and travelling late on the Underground.

If by any chance – and it seemed a slim one – you did survive intact, clearly something nice must happen, otherwise the information wouldn't be D-noticed. But what, precisely? And how to find out?

Parents were obviously unreliable: double agents who got blown early on when trying to feed you some deliberate piece of misinformation. My own had been tossed an easy enough question – to which I naturally already knew the answer – and had botched their response. Reading the Bible for prep one evening, I hustled my mother's mind out of the *She* competition page with

'Mummy, what's an oonuch?'

'Oh, I'm not sure, dear, really,' she answered in a level voice. (It could just be true that she wasn't.) 'Let's ask your father. Jack, Christopher wants to know what a eunuch is ... ' (Good play that, correcting pronunciation but disguising knowledge.) My father looked up from his accountancy magazine (didn't he get enough of that stuff at work?), paused, ran his hand over his bald scalp, paused, took off his glasses, paused. All this time he was looking at my mother (had the Big Moment come?); all the same time I was pretending to glare at my Bible, as if vigorous examination of the context would answer my query. My father had just opened his mouth when my mother went on, in her shop voice

' ... it's a sort of Abyssinian servant, I think, isn't it, dear?' I sensed that they were looking hard at each other. Suspicions confirmed, I scrammed as fast as possible:

'Oh I see, yes, that fits the context ... thanks.'

Another alley sealed off. School, where in theory you learned things, wasn't much help either. Colonel Lowson, the jumpy biology master whom we despised because he'd apologised to a boy after hitting him, had a red face anyway; but we were sure he would have blushed, had he been able, when twice a week for a whole term, we responded to his automatic 'Any questions?' at the end of the lesson with

'When are we going to do human reproduction, sir, it's on the syllabus?'

We knew we had him there. Gilchrist, one of the form slickers, had got hold of the examining board syllabus and discovered the undeniable truth. The end of the General Science (Biology) course read: REPRODUCTION: PLANT, RABBIT, HUMAN. We monitored Lowson's pedestrian progress through the course like Indian scouts watching a suicidally predictable troop of US Cavalry. Finally, there remained only two words left undiscussed on the whole syllabus – RABBIT, HUMAN – and two lessons left. Lowson had ridden into a box canyon.

'Next week,' Lowson began the first of these two final lessons, 'I shall be doing revision … '

'Ruined,' sang out Gilchrist softly, and a disappointed murmur ran through the class.

' … but today I'm going to be dealing with reproduction in mammals.' Silence; one or two of us got hard-ons at the prospect. Lowson knew he wouldn't have any trouble that day; and, while we took more notes than ever before, he told us about rabbits, partly in Latin. It didn't, to be honest, sound much of a Big Deal. It obviously couldn't be *exactly* the same. Surely the bit where … But then we began to realise that Lowson was getting away with it. Almost the entire forty-five minutes had gone. Our mounting discontent was evident. Finally, with a minute left:

'Well, any questions?'

'Sir, whennawe gonnado humreprdctionsir, onnasyllabus?'

'Ah,' he replied (and did we detect a smirk?), 'it's just the same principle as in other mammals.' Then he marched out of the room.

Elsewhere in the school, information was just as hard to come by, at least through official channels. The article on family planning in the 'Home' volume of the big encyclopaedia had been ripped out of the school library copy. The only other source of knowledge was much too risky – the Headmaster's confirmation class. This contained a brief session on marriage 'which you won't need just yet but won't do you any harm to know about'. There was indeed no harm in it: the most exciting phrase used by the gaunt and suspicious ruler of our lives was 'mutual comfort and companionship'. At the end of the session, he indicated a pile of booklets on the corner of his desk.

'Anyone who wants to know more can borrow one of these as he goes out.'

He might as well have said, 'Hands up those who abuse their bodies more than six times a day.' I never saw anyone take a booklet. I never knew anyone who'd taken one. I never knew of anyone who knew of anyone who'd taken one. In all probability, simply slowing down as you passed the Headmaster's desk was a beating offence.

We were left, as Toni frequently put it, to our own vices; and what we came up with was scrappy indeed. You couldn't just ask other boys – like John Pepper, who claimed to have 'had' a married woman, or Fuzz Woolley, whose diary was full of red-ink crosses which supposedly represented the dates of his girl friend's periods. You couldn't ask, because all jokes and conversations on the subject implied mutual and equal knowledge; to admit ignorance would have undefined but dreadful consequences – like those of failing to pass on a chain letter.

We had some grasp of the main event – even Lowson's scanty briefing had left us with the concept of intromission; but the actual logistics of the matter were still hazy. Of more immediate and basic concern was what a woman's body actually looked like. We relied a lot on the *National Geographic Magazine*, required reading for the school intellectuals; though it was sometimes hard to extrapolate much from a pygmy woman with patterned tattoo scars, body paint and a loincloth. Bra and corset ads, posters for X-films, and Sir William Orpen's *History of Art* all chipped in a little. But it wasn't until Brian Stiles pulled out his copy of *Span*, a pocket-sized nudist mag (stablemate of *Spick*), that things became a little clearer. So *that*'s what it's like, we thought, gazing at the air-brushed lower belly of a female trampolinist.

Though unremittingly carnal, we were also deeply idealistic. It felt like a pretty good mixture. We couldn't bear Racine because, though the strength of emotion experienced by his characters was, we reckoned, probably about the same as we would undergo in our turn, the daisy-chains of passion on which his plots turned disgusted us. Corneille was our man; or rather, his women were our women – passionate yet dutiful, faithful and virginal. Toni and I debated the woman question a lot; though it rarely got off a familiar track.

'So, we have to marry virgins?' (It made no difference which of us began.)

'Well, you don't have to; but if you marry someone who isn't a virgin she may turn out to be a nympho.'

'But if you marry a virgin she may turn out to be frigid?'

'Well, if she's frigid, you can always get a divorce and start again.'

'Whereas … '

' … whereas if she's a nympho, you can't very well go to a judge and say she's not letting you. You're stuck with it. You'd be … '

' … roooiined. Quite.'

We thought of Shakespeare, Molière, and other authorities. They all agreed that the ridiculous husband was not something to be laughed at.

'So, it has to be a virgin.'

'It has to be.'

And we'd shake hands on it.

But our practical steps towards girls were more halting than our decisions of principle. How did you tell a nympho? How did you tell a virgin? How – hardest of all – did you tell a wife: someone who looked like a nympho but was actually a virgin.

Most evenings, on our way home, Toni and I would eye a couple of chippies from the girls' school who were usually waiting on Temple Underground station for the same train as us. Magenta uniforms, neat black hair both of them, and *real stockings*. Their school was just over the road from us, but sororisation was discouraged. They were even let out a quarter of an hour before us, so that they could get clear of … what? And what did the girls themselves think they were being allowed to get clear of? *Ergo*, any girls travelling on the same train as us had obviously waited around solely in order to travel on the same train as us. *Ergo* they wanted us to approach them. *Ergo*, they were potential nymphos. *Ergo*, Toni and I refused to return their shy smiles.

4 · The Constructive Loaf

Wednesday afternoons were always half-day holidays. 12.30, and a scatter of boys stuffing caps into satchels debouched from the side entrance of the High Victorian building on the Embankment; a few minutes later, a more sedate file of capless sixth-formers would saunter down the front steps, swinging their umbrellas casually. On Wednesdays, the History Society would run improving trips to Hatfield House; the CCF fanatics would grease their bayonets; boys would head off with a Swiss roll of towel under their arms, with foils, cricket bags, rancid fives gloves. The timid would make a dash for home, reasonably sure that rapists and castrators were not yet abroad on the Underground.

Toni and I indulged in the Constructive Loaf. London, we had read somewhere, combined everything you could require. There was, of course, Travel as well, and we intended doing some of that later (even though we'd both been to the country and found it disappointingly empty), because all our authorities agreed that it was good for the brain. But London was where you started from; and it was to London that, finally, stuffed with wisdom, you returned. And the way to crack London's secrets was the Loaf. *Il vaut mieux gâcher sa jeunesse que de n'en rien faire.*

It was Toni who first put forward the concept of the Constructive Loaf. Our time, he argued, was spent being either compulsorily crammed with knowledge, or compulsorily diverted. His theory was that by lounging about in a suitably *insouciant* fashion, but keeping an eye open all the time, you could really catch life on the hip – you could harvest all the *aperçus* of the *flâneur*. Also, we liked loafing around and watching other people doing things and tiring themselves. We went to the alleys off Fleet Street to see gross rolls of newsprint being unloaded. We went to street markets and law courts, hovered outside pubs and bra-shops. We went to St Paul's with our binoculars, ostensibly to examine the frescoes and mosaics of the dome, but actually to focus on people praying. We searched for prostitutes – the only other constructive loafers there were, we wittily thought – who in those days were still identifiable by a delicate gold chain round the ankle. We would ask each other,

'Do you think she's plying for trade?'

We didn't actually do anything except observe; though Toni was accosted one moist and foggy afternoon by a myopic (or desperate) whore. He answered her businesslike

'How about it then, love?'

with a confident if piccolo-voiced

'How much will you pay me?'

and claimed an épat.

'Disqualified.'

'Why?'

'You can't *épater la Bohème*. It's ridiculous.'

'Why not? Whores are an integral part of bourgeois life. Remember your Maupassant. It's like dogs taking after their masters: whores take on the petty values and rigidity of their clients.'

'False analogy – the clients are the dogs, the whores are the mistresses ... '

'Doesn't matter as long as you admit the principle of mutual influence ... '

Then we both realised that neither of us had noticed how the long-gone chippy had reacted. It was no épat if she'd liked the joke.

This sort of contact, however, was deemed unrewarding. We preferred not to talk to people, as this got in the way of our observation of them. If asked specifically what we were looking for, we'd probably have said, 'Rimbaud's *musique savante de la ville*'. We wanted scenes, things, people, as if filling one of Big Chief I-Spy's little books – but our book was not yet written, for it was only when we saw what we saw that we knew we were looking for it. Certain things were ideal and unattainable – like walking in spectral gas-light across damp cobblestones and hearing the distant cry of a barrel-organ – but we hunted jumpily for the original, the picturesque, the authentic.

We hunted emotions. Railway termini gave us weepy fare-wells and coarse recouplings. That was easy. Churches gave us the vivid deceptions of faith – though we had to be careful in our manner of observation. Harley Street doorsteps gave us, we believed, the rabbit fears of men about to die. And the National Gallery, our most frequent haunt, gave us examples of pure aesthetic pleasure – although, to be honest, they weren't as frequent, as pure, or as subtle as we'd first hoped. Out-rageously often, we thought, the scene was one more appropriate to Waterloo or Victoria: people greeted Monet, or Seurat, or Goya as if they had just stepped off a train – 'Well, what a nice surprise. I knew you'd be here, of course, but it's a nice surprise all the same. And my, aren't you looking just as well as ever? Hardly a day older. No really ... '

Our reason for constantly visiting the Gallery was straight-forward. We agreed – indeed, no sane friend of ours would bother to argue – that Art was the most important thing in life, the constant to which one could be unfailingly devoted and which would never cease to reward; more crucially, it was the stuff whose effect on those exposed to it was ameliorative. It made people not just fitter for friendship and more civilised (we saw the circularity of *that*), but *better* – kinder, wiser, nicer, more peaceful, more active, more sensitive. If it didn't, what good was it? Why not just go and suck cornets instead? *Ex hypothesi* (as we would have said, or indeed *ex vero*), the moment someone perceives a work of art he is in some way improved. It seemed quite reasonable to expect that the process could be observed.

To be candid, after a few Wednesdays at the Gallery, we felt a bit like those eighteenth-century physicians who combed battlefields and dissected fresh corpses to track down the seat of the soul. Still, some of them believed they'd got results; and there'd been that Swedish doctor who weighed his terminal patients, hospital bed and all, just before and just after death. Twenty-one grammes, apparently, made the vital difference. We didn't expect any weight changes at the Gallery, but we thought ourselves entitled to something. You must be able to see something. And, at times, you did. But more often you found yourself noting extrinsic reactions, as a weary file of name-gloaters, school-sneerers, frame-freaks, colour-grousers, restoration loons and topographers trooped by. You got to know the quizzical chin-in-hand stance; the manly, combative, hands-on-hips square-up; the eyes-down-on-the-booklet position; the glazed XII-down, XIV-to-go trot. Sometimes, we wondered if we were any the wiser.

Eventually, we were driven reluctantly to testing one another. This we did at Toni's home, in what we judged to be laboratory conditions. This meant that for pictures, we thumbed in ear-plugs; while for music, we bound our eyes with a rugger sock. The experimentee would be given five minutes' exposure to, say, Monet's 'Rouen Cathedral', or the scherzo of Brahms PC2, and then consider his response. He would purse his lips like a wine-bibber and pause reflectively. You had, after all, to axe away all that form-and-content analysis stuff they taught at school. We were after something simpler, truer, deeper, more elemental. So, how did you feel, and what changes would happen if you continued with the prescription?

Toni would always answer with his eyes closed, even after a pic. He would frown until his eyebrows met, wash a quiet 'Mnnnnn' round his mouth for a bit, and then deliver:

'Skin tension, mainly in legs and arms. Thighs rippling. Exhilaration, yes I think that's right. Aspiring thorax. Confidence. Not smugness, though. More a sort of firm bonhomie. Up to an amiable épat, at least.'

I'd note all this down in our ledger, on a right-hand page.

The left already contained the source of the inspiration: 'Glinka, R. & Lud. ov. Reiner/Chi SO/RCA Victrola; 9/12/63.'

It was all part of our drive towards helping the world understand itself.

5 · J'habite Metroland

'Rootless.'

'*Sans racines.*'

'*Sans Racine?*'

'The open road? The spiritual vagabond?'

'The bundle of ideas wrapped up in a red spotted handkerchief?'

'*L'adieu suprême d'un mouchoir?*'

Toni and I prided ourselves on being rootless. We also aspired to a future condition of rootlessness, and saw no contradiction in the two states of mind; or in the fact that we each lived with our parents, who were, for that matter, the freeholders of our respective homes.

Toni far outclassed me in rootlessness. His parents were Polish Jews and, though we didn't actually know it for certain, we were practically sure that they had escaped from the Warsaw ghetto at the very last minute. This gave Toni the flash foreign name of Barbarowski, two languages, three cultures, and a sense (he assured me) of atavistic wrench: in short, real class. He looked an exile, too: swarthy, bulbous-nosed, thick-lipped, disarmingly short, energetic and hairy; he even had to shave every day.

Despite the handicaps of being English and non-Jewish, I tried to do my bit in a Home Counties sort of way. Our family was small, but there was enough tepidity of feeling to effect a widish diaspora. The Lloyds (well, our Lloyds, my father's Lloyds at least) came from Basingstoke; my mother's family from Lincoln; relatives skulked incommunicado in several counties, lying low at Christmas, turning up with sulky regularity at funerals, and, if pressed, at weddings. Apart from Uncle Arthur, who lived within Sunday-afternoon distance, they were inaccessible; which suited me fine, as I could pretend they were all picturesque rustics, gnarled artisans or homicidal eccentrics. All they had to do was fork out at Christmas, and fork out money, or at least something that was convertible.

Like Toni, I was dark, but several inches taller; some would have called me skinny, but I preferred to think of myself as having the whippy strength of a young sapling. My nose, I hoped, still had a bit of growing left to do; my cheeks were free of moles; occasionally, a squad of acne would make its listless progress across my forehead; my best feature, I believed, was my eyes – deep, saturnine, full of secrets learned and not yet learned (at least, that was how I saw them).

It was a low-key English face, which suited the low-key sense of expatriation common to all who lived in Eastwick. Everyone in this suburb of a couple of thousand people seemed to have come in from elsewhere. They would have been attracted by the solidly built houses, the reliable railway service, and the good gardening soil. I found the cosy, controlled rootlessness of the place reassuring; though I did tend to complain to Toni that I'd prefer something

' ... more elemental. I wish I were, oh, somewhat more sort of bare and forked.'

'You mean you wish you were somewhat more bare and fugged.'

Well, yes, that too, I suppose; at least I think so.

'*Où habites-tu?*' they would ask year after year, drilling us for French orals; and always I would smirkingly reply,

'*J'habite Metroland.*'

It sounded better than Eastwick, stranger than Middlesex; more like a concept in the mind than a place where you shopped. And so, of course, it was. As the Metropolitan Railway had pushed westward in the 1880s, a thin corridor of land was opened up with no geographical or ideological unity: you lived there because it was an area easy to get out of. The name Metroland – adopted during the First World War both by estate agents and the railway itself – gave the string of rural suburbs a spurious integrity.

In the early 1960s, the Metropolitan Line (by which the purist naturally meant the Watford, Chesham and Amersham branches) still retained some of its original separateness. The rolling-stock, painted a distinctive mid-brown, had remained unchanged for sixty years; some of the bogeys, my Ian Allen spotter's book informed me, had been running since the early 1890s. The carriages were high and square, with broad wooden running-boards; the compartments were luxuriously wide by modern standards, and the breadth of the seats made one marvel at Edwardian femural development. The backs of the seats were raked at an angle which implied that in the old days the trains had stopped for longer at the stations.

Above the seats were sepia photographs of the line's beauty spots – Sandy Lodge Golf Course, Pinner Hill, Moor Park, Chorleywood. Most of the original fittings remained: wide, loosely strung luggage racks with coat-hooks curving down from their support struts; broad leather window straps, and broad leather straps to stop the doors from swinging all the way back on their hinges; a chunky, gilded figure on the door, 1 or 3; a brass fingerplate backing the brass door handle; and, engraved on the plate, in a tone of either command or seductive invitation, the slogan 'Live in Metroland'.

Over the years I studied the rolling stock. From the platform I could tell at a glance a wide from an extra-wide compartment. I knew all the advertisements by heart, and all the varieties of decoration on the barrel-vaulted ceilings. I knew the range of imagination of the people who scraped the NO SMOKING transfers on the windows into new mottoes: NO SNORING was the most popular piece of knife-work; NO SNOGING a baffler for years; NO SNOWING the most whimsical. I stowed away in a first-class carriage one dark afternoon, and sat bolt upright in the soft seat, too frightened to look around me. I even penetrated, by mistake, the special single compartment at the front of each train, which was protected by a green transfer: LADIES ONLY. Having only just caught my connection, I fell panting into the silent disapproval of three tweeded ladies; though my fear was cooled less by their silence than by my disappointment that the compartment contained no special appurtenances indicative, however obliquely, of just what it was that made women different.

One afternoon, rolling home as usual on the 4.13 from Baker Street, I had finished my prep and my thoughts, and was staring at the purply-red skeleton map of the line, which occupied the central slot beneath the luggage-rack. I was checking off the stations like rosary-beads when a voice on my right said

'Verney Junction.'

He was an old sod, I thought; dead bourgeois. The embroidered sun shining out of his slippers was the nearest *he* got to energy and life, I thought. Bet he was *syphilisé*. Pity he wasn't Belgian. He might be Belgian. What had he said?

'Verney Junction,' he repeated. 'Quainton Road. Winslow Road. Grandborough Road. Waddesdon. Never heard of them,' he stated, sure that I hadn't. Old sod. Well, too old to hate really. Commuter's uniform; umbrella with a gold spoke-ring; brief-case; looking-glass shoes. The brief-case probably contained portable Nazi X-ray equipment.

'No.'

'Used to be a great line. Used to have … ambitions. Heard of the Brill Line?' What was he after? Rape, abduction? Better humour him, otherwise six months and I'd be plump and ball-less in Turkey.

'No.'

'Brill Line from Quainton Road. All the Ws. Waddesdon Road. Wescott. Wotton. Wood Siding. Brill. Built by the Duke of Buckingham. Imagine that. Had it built for his own estate, you see. Part of the Metropolitan Line for thirty years now. Do you know, I went on the last train. 1935, '36, something like that. Last train from Brill to Verney Junction. Sounds like a film, doesn't it?'

Not one that I'd go to see. And certainly not if he asked me. He must be a rapist; anyone who spoke to kids on trains obviously was, *ex hypothesi*. But he was a rickety old fugger, and I was on the platform side of the train. Also, I had my umbrella. Better talk him out of it. They sometimes turn nasty if you don't talk to them.

'Ever been first class?' Should I call him Sir?

'This was a grand line, you know. The Extension Line they used to call it' (was he getting dirty?) 'this part out from Baker Street to Verney Junction. There used to be a Pullman car' (was he getting round to my question?) 'right up until Hitler's war started. Two Pullman cars in fact. Imagine – imagine a Pullman car on the Bakerloo Line.' (He laughed contemptuously, I sycophantically) 'Two of them. One was called the *Mayflower*. Can you imagine that? Can't remember what the other one was called.' (He tapped his thigh with a bunch of fingertips; but this didn't help. Was he getting dirty again?) 'No, but the *Mayflower* was one of them. The first Pullman cars in Europe to be hauled by electricity.'

'No, really? The first in Europe?' I was almost as interested as I pretended to be.

'The first in Europe. There's a lot of history in this line, you know. Heard of John Stuart Mill?'

'Yes.' (Of course not)

'Do you know what his last speech in the House was about?' I think I must have shown that I didn't.

'The House of Commons. His last speech? It was about the Underground. Can you imagine that? The Railway Regulation Bill, 1868. An amendment was moved to the bill making it obligatory for all railways to attach a smoking carriage to their trains. Mill got the bill through. Made a great speech in favour of it. Carried the day.'

Jolly good. It was jolly good, wasn't it?

'*But* – guess what – there was one railway, just one, that was exempted. *That* was the Metropolitan.'

You would have thought he'd been down there himself voting in eighteen whatever.

'Why?'

'Ah. Because of the smoke in the tunnels. It's always been a bit special, you see.'

Maybe he wasn't so bad. Only four stations to go anyway. Maybe he was quite interesting.

'What about those other places? Quinton whatsit.'

'Quainton Road. They were all out beyond Aylesbury. Waddesdon, Quainton Road, it went, Grandborough, Winslow Road, Verney Junction.' (If he went on like this, I'd cry) 'Fifty miles from Verney Junction to Baker Street; what a line. Can you imagine – they were planning to join up with Northampton and Birmingham. Have a great link through from Yorkshire and Lancashire, through Quainton Road, through London, joining up with the old South Eastern, then through a Channel Tunnel to the Continent. What a line.'

He paused. An empty school playground flitted by; a metal merry-go-round draped with washing; the flash of a windscreen.

'They never built the Outer Circle either.'

He was an elegiac old fugger, that was for sure. He told me about workmen's fares, and electrification, and Lord's Station, which was closed when war broke out. About someone called Sir Edward Watkin, who had some plans or other; some ambitious old turd, no doubt, who couldn't tell Tissot from Titian.

'It wasn't just ambition, you see. There was confidence as well. Confidence *in* ambition ... Nowadays ... ' He spotted the reflex glaze-over which my face always gave when I heard that last word. 'Don't sneer at the Victorians, my lad,' he said sharply. Suddenly he sounded as if he was turning nasty again; maybe he was a rapist; maybe he realised how I'd outwitted him. 'Look at the things they did instead.'

What, me. sneer at the Victorians? I didn't have enough sneer-room left. By the time I'd finished sneering at dummos, prefects, masters, parents, my brother and sister, Third

Division (North) football, Molière, God, the bourgeoisie and normal people, I didn't have any strength left for more than a twisted pout at history. I looked at the old fugger and had a go at an expression of moral outrage; but it wasn't one my face was much good at.

'You see, it wasn't just the people who built the railway and ran it. It was everyone else as well. You probably aren't interested,' (Christ, he did go on, didn't he?) 'but when the first through train from Baker Street to Farringdon Street arrived, the passengers cleaned out the restaurant buffet at Farringdon Street in ten minutes flat,' (maybe they were hungry because they were scared) 'ten minutes flat. Like a plague of locusts.' He was almost talking to himself now, but I thought it wise to slot in another question, just to be on the safe side.

'Is that when they called it Metroland?' I asked, not really sure when I was talking about, but taking care not to sneer.

'Metroland? That nonsense.' He turned his attention to me again. 'That was the beginning of the end. No, that was much later, some time during the war before Hitler's. That was all to please the estate agents. Make it sound cosy. Cosy homes for cosy heroes. Twenty-five minutes from Baker Street and a pension at the end of the line,' he said unexpectedly. 'Made it what it is now, a bourgeois dormitory.'

It was as if someone had dropped a bag of cutlery inside my head. Hey. Christ. You can't say that. It's not allowed. Look at yourself. *I* can call *you* bourgeois; well, I think I can anyway. You can't call yourself it. It's just not … on. I mean, it's against all the known rules. It's like a master admitting he knows his own nickname. It … well, I suppose it can only be answered by a non-conventional response.

'Aren't you a bourgeois, then?' I inventoried to myself his clothes, voice, briefcase.

'Ha. Of course I am,' he said lightly, almost gently. His tone reassured me; but his words remained a puzzle.

6 · Scorched Earth

Toni and I worked hard at deconditioning. After a thoughtful session of Bruckner ('Lowering of pulse; vague tugging inside chest; occas. shoulder-jerks; foot-twitching. Go out and beat up a queer? Bruckner 4/Philh./Columbia/Klemperer), or when we were too tired to go out for a mild épat, we'd often come back to the same theme.

'One thing about parents. They fug you up.'

'Do you think they mean to?'

'They may not. But they do, don't they?'

'Yeah, but it's not really their fault, is it?'

'You mean like in Zola – because they were fugged up in their turn by their parents.'

'Good point. But you've got to blame them a bit, haven't you? I mean, for not realising they were being fugged up, and going on and doing it to us as well?'

'Oh, sure, I'm not suggesting we shouldn't go on punishing them.'

'You had me worried for a bit.'

Every morning, at breakfast, I would gaze disbelievingly at my family. They were all still there, for a start – that was the first surprise. Why hadn't some of them run off in the night, wounded beyond endurance by the emptiness I divined in their lives? Why were they all still sitting where they'd sat the morning before, and looking as if they'd be perfectly content to be back there again in another twenty-four hours?

Across the table, my elder brother Nigel gazed over the top

of his Weetabix at a science fiction mag. (Maybe this was how he controlled his existential discontent: by escaping into *New Galaxies* and *New Worlds* and *Astounding Realities*. Not that I'd ever asked him if he suffered from existential discontent; if anything, I rather hoped he didn't – these things can get too popular.) Next to him, my sister Mary was also staring over the top of her breakfast, reading the pepper and salt. It wasn't because she hadn't yet woken up properly: at dinner she read the knives and forks. One day she might graduate to the backs of cornflake packets. She was thirteen and didn't talk much. I thought she looked more like Nigel than me: they both had bland, soft-featured, unresentful faces.

On my right, my father had *The Times* folded back at the stock-exchange prices and was murmuring his way down them. He didn't look like me either. For a start, he was bald. I suppose the cast of his jaw was a bit like mine, but he certainly didn't have my profound, questing eyes. From time to time he would toss my mother a dutiful question about the garden. She sat on my left, brought the food, answered any questions, and chivvied us gently through the largely silent meal. I didn't look like her either. Some people said I had her eyes; but even if I did, I didn't have anything else.

Could it be that I was really related to all of them? And how could I bear not to point out the obvious differences?

'Mum, am I illegitimate?' (Normal conversational pitch)

I heard a slight rustle to my left. Both my siblings carried on with their reading.

'No, dear. Got your sandwiches?'

'Yeah. You sure there isn't a chance I'm illegitimate?' I waved an explicatory hand towards Nigel and Mary. My father cleared his throat quietly.

'School, Christopher.'

Well, they could be lying.

Parenthood, for Toni and me, was a crime of strict liability. There didn't need to be any *mens rea*, just the *actus reus* of birth. The sentence we doled out, after giving due consideration to all the circumstances of the case and the social background of

the offenders, was one of perpetual probation. And as for ourselves, the victims, the *mal-aimés*, we realised that independent
existence could only be achieved by strict deconditioning.
Camus had left everyone else on the grid with his '*Aujourd'hui
Maman est morte. Ou peut-être hier.*' Deconning, as we called it,
savouring the pun, was the duty of every self-respecting
adolescent.

But it was harder than we reckoned. There were, we worked
out, two distinct stages. First came Scorched Earth – syste-
matic rejection, wilful contradiction, a wide-ranging, anarchic
slate-wipe. After all, we were part of the Anger generation.

'Do you realise,' I said to Toni one lunchtime, as we were
loafing rather unconstructively on the sixth-form balcony,
'that we're part of the Anger generation?'

'Yeah, I'm really cross about it.' His familiar squint-
grin.

'And that when we're old and have … nephews and nieces,
they're going to ask us what we did in the Great Anger?'

'Well, we're in there, aren't we, being Angry?'

'Isn't it a bit off, though, that we're reading Osborne at
school with old Runcaster? I mean, don't you think some sort
of institutionalisation might be going on?'

'What d'you mean?'

'Well, heading off the revolt of the intelligentsia by trying to
absorb it into the body politic.'

'So?'

'So, I just thought, maybe the real action's in Complacency.'

'Scholasticism,' Toni sneered comfortingly. 'Pinhead-
dancer.'

The trouble was, he had a much cushier time being Angry
than I did. Toni's parents (partly, we guessed, because of their
ghetto experiences) were (a) religious, (b) disciplinarian, (c)
possessively loving, and (d) poor. All he had to be was an idle,
agnostic, independent spendthrift, and there he was – Angry.
Only the previous year he had broken a door handle at home,
and his father had stopped his pocket money for three weeks.
That sort of gesture was really helpful. Whereas when I was

destructive, petulant or obstinate, my parents, shamefully well-heeled in tolerance, would merely identify my condition for me ('It's always a tricky time, Christopher, growing up'). That identification was the nearest I could get them to come towards reproach. I'd be in there, jabbing away; I'd throw a feint, then sink one right in up to the wrist – and what would my mother do? Get out the iodine and lint for my knuckles.

Scorched Earth didn't go the whole way, of course. With a perspicacity beyond our years, we appreciated that merely rejecting or reversing the outlook and morality of one's parents was scarcely more than a coarse reflex response. Just as blasphemy implies religion, we argued, so a blanket expungement of childhood impositions indicates some endorsement of them. And we couldn't have that. So, without in any way compromising our principles, we agreed to carry on living at home.

Scorched Earth was part one; part two was Reconstruction. This was on the schedule, anyway; though there were many good reasons, and good metaphors, to back up our reluctance to look at that part of things too closely.

'What about Reconstruction?'

'What about it?'

'Do you think we ought to plan for it a bit?'

'That's what we're doing now – that's what SE's about.'

'Mmmnnn.'

'I mean, I don't think we should commit ourselves too strongly at this stage to any particular line. We are only sixteen after all.'

That was true enough. Life didn't really get under way until you left school; we were mature enough to acknowledge this point. When you did get out there, you started

' … making Moral Decisions … '

' … and Having Relationships … '

' … and Becoming Famous … '

' … and Choosing Your Own Clothes … '

For the moment, though, all you could do in these areas was

judge your parents, associate with the confidants of your hates, try to become well-known to smaller boys without actually talking to them, and decide between a single and a double Windsor. It didn't add up to much.

7 · *Mendacity Curves*

Sunday was the day for which Metroland was created. On Sunday mornings, as I lay in bed wondering how to kill the day, two sounds rang out across the silent, contented suburb: the church bells and the train. The bells nagged you awake, persisted with irritating stamina, and finally gave up with a defeated half-clunk. The trains clattered more loudly than usual into Eastwick station, as if celebrating their lack of passengers. It wasn't until the afternoon – by some tacit but undisputed agreement – that a third noise started up: the patterned roar of motor mowers, accelerating, braking, turning, accelerating, braking, turning. When they fell silent, you might catch the quiet chomp of shears; and finally – a sound absorbed rather than heard – the gentle squeak of chamois on boot and bonnet.

It was the day of garden hoses (we all paid extra on the rates for an outside tap); of yahoo kids shouting dementedly from several gardens away; of beachballs rising above the level of the fence; of learner drivers panicking on three-point turns in the road outside; of young men taking the family car up to The Stile for a drink before lunch, and dropping their blue salt papers through the slats of the teak gardenware. Sundays, it seemed, were always peaceful, and always sunny.

I loathed them, with all the rage of one continuously disappointed to discover that he is not self-sufficient. I loathed the Sunday papers, which tried to fill your dozing brain with thoughts you didn't want; I loathed the Sunday radio, spilling over with arid critics; I loathed the Sunday television, all Brains Trust and serious plays about grown-ups and emotional crises and nuclear war and that sort of stuff. I loathed staying in, while the sun crept furtively round the room and suddenly hit you smack in the eyes; and sitting out, when the same sun liquefied your brain and sent it slopping round your skull. I loathed Sunday's tasks – swabbing down the car, with soapy water running upwards (how did it do that?) into your armpit; emptying the grass-cuttings and scraping your nails on the bottom of the metal barrow. I loathed working, and not working; going for walks over the golf course and meeting other people going for walks over the golf course; and doing what you did most, which was wait for Monday.

The only break in the routine of Sundays came when my mother announced,

'We're going to see Uncle Arthur this afternoon.'

'Why?' The ritual objection was always worth registering. It never got anywhere, and I didn't mind that it didn't; I just felt that Nigel and Mary might benefit from the example of independent thinking.

'Because he's your uncle.'

'He'll still be my uncle next weekend; and the weekend after that.'

'That's not the point. We haven't been over for eight weeks or so.'

'How do you know he wants to see us?'

'Of course he wants to see us – we haven't been over for two months.'

'Did he ring up and ask to see us?'

'Of course he didn't; you know he never does.' (Too mean)

'Then how do you know he wants to see us?'

'Because he always wants to see us after this sort of time. Now don't be aggravating, Christopher.'

'But he might be reading a book or doing something interesting.'

'Well, I'd drop a book to see a relation I hadn't seen for two months.'

'I wouldn't.'

'Well, that's hardly the point, Christopher.'

'What is the point?' (Nigel yawning ostentatiously by this time)

'The point is we're going over there this afternoon. Now go and wash for lunch.'

'Can I take a book?'

'Well, you can take one to read in the car; but you'll have to leave it in the car. It's rude to go visiting with a book.'

'Isn't it rude to go visiting when you don't really want to go visiting?'

'Christopher, go and wash.'

'Can I take a book to the bathroom?'

And so on. I could prolong these conversations indefinitely without exhausting my mother's patience; her only indication of disapproval was to call me by my name. She knew I would be going. I did too.

As soon as the washing-up was over, we climbed into our chunky Morris Oxford, black with plum upholstery. Mary would stare vacuously out of the window and let her hair be blown over her face without brushing it away. Nigel bent over a mag. I used to hum and whistle, always starting off with a Guy Béart song I'd heard on long wave, whose first line was *'Cerceuil à roulettes, tombeau à moteur'*. This was partly to make myself uncheerful, and partly a protest against the Front Seat's refusal to use the Motorola. It had come with the car and was, in my view, the chief selling point of this non-foreign, non-streamlined, non-red, non-sports car. There was even a sticker in the back window, which had resisted various applications of soapy water, advertising the Motorola: it read I'VE BEEN EXPOSED TO RADIO ACTIVITY. We weren't allowed to use it on the road, because, the Front Seat maintained, it would be distracting to the driver (and we weren't allowed to use it in the garage because that ran down the battery).

Twenty minutes of safe driving brought us to Uncle Arthur's bungalow near Chesham. He was a humorous old fugger – cunning, stingy, and usually lying. He lied in a way I always found engaging: not for profit, or even for effect, but simply because it gave him a thrill. Toni and I had once done a pilot study of lying, and after a thorough examination of everyone we knew had plotted a Mendacity Curve on a piece of graph paper. It looked like the horizontal cross-section of a pair of tits, with the nipples at ages sixteen and sixty. Arthur and I were probably peaking at just about the same time.

'Hullo all,' he shouted as we turned into the drive. He was white-haired, stooped more than he needed to because it gained him unearned sympathy, and dressed with an aggressive scruffiness designed to make you feel sorry for his bachelor life. My theory was that he'd only remained unmarried because there was no one rich enough to keep him who was also stupid enough not to see through him. 'Did you make good time?'

'Not too bad, Arthur,' replied my father, winding up his window. 'Bit of a hold-up at Four Roads, but I suppose you've got to expect that.'

'Yes, bloody Sunday motorists. Oops, excuse my French.' Arthur had just pretended to spot me getting out of the car. 'And how are you, lad? Brought some reading I see.' It was a small pocket edition of Flaubert's *Dictionnaire des Idées Reçues*.

'Yes, Uncle, I knew you wouldn't mind.' (With a half-glance at my mother)

'Of course not, course not. Need a bit of help, first, though.'

Uh-huh.

Melodramatically, Arthur straightened up his back with his thickened fingers, then kneaded away at the cable-stitches of his cardigan as if they were strings of seized-up muscles.

'Been having a bit of trouble with a stump out back. Come and have a look. Why don't the rest of you go in?' (Nigel was always spared chores like this because of an obscure chest complaint; Mary on the grounds of being a girl; my parents on the grounds of being parents.)

Still, I had to admire the old sod. If his back was playing up, it must have been because some chair-cushions had turned nasty on it. He knew better than to go digging up stumps so soon after Sunday lunch. Half an hour with the show page of the *Sunday Express* was about all the exercise he'd have taken. But it was all part of an elaborate revenge Arthur had been taking on me for years. During my age of innocence, he'd met us one Sunday with some tale about shagging himself out in the garden. While he was boring on to my father about brassica, I'd whipped into the lounge and given his chair a quiet feel. Hot as goose-shit, just as I'd thought. When the others came in I'd casually remarked,

'Uncle, you can't have been digging the garden like you said – your chair's still warm.'

He'd scanned me with an unforgiving glance, then rushed off with an energy untypical of one who'd just been tangling with cabbage stumps. 'Ferdinand,' we'd heard him shouting. 'Ferdinand. FERDINAND!!' From the hall, a friendly pad of paws, some slobbery mouth-noises, a solid crump as brogue hit labrador. 'And never let me catch you in my chair again.'

Ever afterwards I would find that Arthur had stored up some small but unpleasant task for me, like turning an inaccessible lug to let the sump-oil out of his car ('*Do* mind your clothes, lad'), or clearing patches of nettles ('Sorry about the gloves, lad, they seem to have rather a lot of holes in them'), or nipping down to catch the post ('You'll have to run there in order to catch it – tell you what, I'll time you.' This was a mistake: I got my own back by walking there, missing the post, and running back). This time it was an enormous fugging tree-stump. Arthur had grazed a shallow trench round it, laid bare a few thin, unimportant rootlets, and deliberately piled some loose earth over a huge root as thick as a thigh.

'Shouldn't give you much trouble, lad. Not unless there's a tap down deep, of course.'

'There's that big one you've covered up as well,' I said. When we were alone together we came close to owning up. I liked him.

'Covered up, whaddya mean, son? That? Is there a root under there? My, my. You'd never think a stump like that would need so many roots, would you? Still, I'm sure an intellectual young chappie like yourself will be able to puzzle it out. By the way, the head does tend to fly off the pick every now and then. See you for tea. My, it is getting chilly.' And he wandered off.

There were various incompetence ploys open to me. There was throwing-the-earth-all-over-the-place- (like on to the lettuce cloches) -in-a-fit-of-enthusiasm. There was breaking-the-tools; though this led to trouble with my father. The best one I thought of – though had to abandon as I couldn't find a bow-saw – was cutting the stump off at ground level and covering the whole thing up with earth ('Oh, sorry, Uncle, you didn't say you wanted me to dig the whole area up – I thought you just wanted to avoid tripping over it in the dark').

Finally, as a compromise, I decided on delaying tactics. I dug in a wide circle of radius four feet or so, all round the stump, occasionally cutting off the odd spindly, unimportant root, but never remotely threatening the solidity of the thing. I worked parodically, with a maniac zest, ignoring four o'clock and finally drawing my uncle out into the garden again.

'Don't catch cold,' I shouted as he approached, 'it's chilly out here if you're not working.'

'Just come to see if you've finished. Christ Albloodymighty, what d'you think you're doing, you berk?' I had by this time sunk a trench a foot wide and nearly three spits deep all round the stump.

'Sapping it, Uncle,' I explained in a professional tone. 'After what you said about the tap-root, I thought I'd better dig wide and deep to start with. I've got those out so far,' I said proudly, pointing to a tiny pile of twig-like roots.

'Bloody Ruskin,' my uncle shouted at me, 'bloody little intellectual wanker. Give you a pig's arse you wouldn't know what to do with it, would you, son?'

'Is tea ready, Uncle?' I asked politely.

After tea, which I used to spend watching hopefully for Arthur's over-dunked ginger-nut to cascade down his cardigan, I got down to some quiet erectile browsing in the garage. In those days, you didn't just dream about sex almost all the time, you also got hard at the slightest provocation. Travelling to school, I'd often have to pull my satchel over my thighs and frenziedly conjugate something to myself in an attempt to get the tumour down by Baker Street. Small-ads for ex-WRAC bloomers, pseudo-histories of Roman circuses, even the *Demoiselles d'Avignon* for Christ's sake: they all worked, all had me digging in my trouser pocket to make readjustments.

The attraction of Arthur's garage was his neatly strung bundles of the *Daily Express*. Arthur Saved Things. I expect it started during the war and was justified by his usual dog-leg logic. He probably thought tying up your newspapers was a slightly less tiring form of digging for victory. Still, I didn't complain. While the grown-ups got down to discussing mortgages and planting-out and tappets, while Mary and Nigel were 'allowed' to do the washing-up, I lolled like a pasha in Arthur's collapsing garage armchair with three dozen copies of the *Express*. 'This America' was the juiciest column in my connoisseur's opinion, with at least one sex story a day; next came the film reviews, the gossip column (posh adulteries got me going), the occasional Ian Fleming serialisation, and cases of rape, incest, exposure and indecent behaviour. I lapped up this version of the life to come with the sheets tented over my knees. You couldn't get up to tricks on these occasions; but in any case the scene was cosy rather than orgasmic. It also gave me lots of material to swap with Gould, whose father always let him read the *News of the World* in the hope that this would let him out of telling his son the facts of life.

'Getting on all right, are we? Sitting comfortably?'

The old fugger had deliberately sneaked in quietly. Still, there's nothing like a surprise for making you lose your hard, and I wasn't troubled on that score.

'Sorry to interrupt, lad, but I thought you wouldn't mind giving me a hand getting some stuff down from the loft. It's rather difficult spotting all the nails in the floor, and I know your eyesight's better than mine.'

8 · Sex, Austerity, War, Austerity

One of the things that would change, when you were Out There Living, would be the sort of notebooks you kept. You wouldn't be writing down what you didn't like doing, or what you'd wished you'd done but hadn't, or what you planned to do in the future; instead, you'd be writing down what you actually did. And since you would only do what you wanted to do, your Deeds Book would read like your Fantasy Book did now, only with a heart-stopping change of tense.

'You know,' I remember saying to Toni one evening, after some ('pulse down, tolerance and benevolence raised, sense of civic place, cerebral cleansing') Vivaldi, 'it's really not a bad time to be, *comment le dire*, young.'

'Nnnnaa?'

'Well, no war. No National Service. More women around than men. No secret police. Getting away with books like *Lady C*. Not bad.'

'You've never had it, Osgood.' (Toni liked to invent misprints)

'No, really. I think it'll be great once we get out.'

'I think you're probably right. Do you see they're calling them the Sexy Sixties already?'

'Sexy, saucy Sixties.' You almost got hard at the sound.

'I suppose it all happens in cycles.'

'What?'

'Well, sex for a start. They had a lot of it in the Twenties as well. It probably all goes in cycles, like: Twenties, Thirties,

Forties, Fifties – Sex, Austerity, War, Austerity; Sixties, Seventies, Eighties, Nineties – Sex, Austerity, War, Austerity?'

Toni cocked an eyebrow. Put like that, it didn't sound too big a deal.

'Which gives us,' I interpreted, 'eight years of sauciness, then a thirty-year wait, with a chance of being killed in the middle. Terrific.'

'Still,' said Toni, determined not to be downcast, 'what could we do in eight years?'

'*Who* could we do in eight years?'

'Just think, though, it could be worse. If you were born in 1915, by the time you were up to it, there'd be Austerity; after that you might get killed; and by the time you got any, you'd be forty-five.'

'You'd have to get married, wouldn't you?'

'There were Army brothels.'

'What if you were in the Navy?'

It did seem as if our parents' generation had been very unlucky.

'Well, we can't help the way their cookie crumbled.'

'Do you think we ought to be nicer to them?'

But it didn't really work out like that. As my Complaints Book proved, every year was full of the same landlocked desires, the same gangrenous resentments, the same modes of inactivity. They say that adolescence is a dynamic period, the mind and body thrusting forward to new discoveries all the time. I don't remember it like that. It all seemed remarkably static. Each year new curricula were fed us, which closely resembled the old curricula; each year a few more people sirred us; each year we were allowed to stay up a bit later on Saturday evenings. But none of the structures changed; power and irresponsibility resided where they always had; the levels of love, awe and resentment remained the same.

'Eight years, then.'

Somehow, it didn't seem very long.

9 · Big D

There were a few private things which I didn't confide to Toni.
Actually, only one: the thing about dying. We always laughed
about it, except on the rare occasions when we knew the person
involved. Lucas, for instance, wing-forward in the Thirds, was
found one morning by his mother, gassed. But even then,
we were more interested in the rumours than in the fact of
his death. A girl friend? The family way? Unable to face
parents?

There must, I suppose, have been some causal connection
between the arrival in my head of the fear of Big D, and the
departure of God; but if so, it was a loose exchange, with no
formal process of reasoning present. God, who had turned up
in my life a decade earlier without proof or argument, got the
boot for a number of reasons, none of which, I suspect, will
seem wholly sufficient: the boringness of Sundays, the creeps
who took it all seriously at school, Baudelaire and Rimbaud,
the pleasure of blasphemy (dangerous, this one), hymn-singing
and organ music and the language of prayer, inability any
longer to think of wanking as a sin, and – as a clincher – an
unwillingness to believe that dead relatives were watching
what I was doing.

So, the whole package had to go, though its loss diminished
neither the boringness of Sundays nor the guilt of wanking.
Within weeks, however, as if to punish me, the infrequent but
paralysing horror of Big D invaded my life. I don't claim any
originality for the timing and location of my bouts of fear

(when in bed, unable to sleep), but I do claim one touch of particularity. The fear of death would always arrive while I was lying on my right side, facing out towards the window and the distant railway line. It would never come when I was on my left side, facing my bookshelves and the rest of the house. Once started, the fear could not be diminished by simply turning over: it had to be played out to the end. To this day, I have a preference for sleeping on my left side.

What was the fear like? Is it different for other people? I don't know. A sudden, rising terror which takes you unawares; a surging need to scream, which the house rules forbid (they always do), so that you lie there with your mouth open in a trembling panic; total wakefulness, which takes an hour or so to subside; and all this as background to and symptom of the central image, part-visual, part-intellectual, of nonexistence. A picture of endlessly retreating stars, taken I expect – with the crass bathos of the unconscious – from the opening credits of a Universal Pictures film; a sensation of total aloneness within your pyjamaed, shaking body; a realisation of Time (always capitalised) going on without you for ever and ever; and a persecuted sense of having been trapped into the present situation by person or persons unknown.

The fear of dying meant, of course, not the fear of dying but the fear of being dead. Few fallacies depressed me more than the line: 'I don't mind being dead; it's just like being asleep. It's the dying I can't face.' Nothing seemed clearer to me in my nocturnal terrors than that death bore no resemblance to sleep. I wouldn't mind Dying at all, I thought, as long as I didn't end up Dead at the end of it.

While Toni and I never discussed basic fears, concepts of immortality naturally came under discussion. Like self-respecting maze-rats, we looked for ways out. There was partial survival to be considered – a gruelly bit of essence nimbusing around in a Huxleyan goo – but we didn't go much on that. There was immortality through one's children; but looking at how we represented our own parents, we couldn't be sanguine about our own chances of surrogate survival when it came to our turn. Mostly, in our sneaky, whining dreams of immortality, we concentrated on art.

> *Tout passe. — L'art robuste*
> *Seul a l'éternité.*

It was all laid out for us there, in the last poem of *Emaux et Camées*. Gautier was a comforting sort of hero. There was no messing with him. He looked tough as well – like a grizzled prop-forward; he'd had lots of women, too. And he said things in ways we could follow without notes.

> *Les dieux eux-mêmes meurent.*
> *Mais les vers souverains*
> *Demeurent*
> *Plus forts que les airains.*

Belief in art was initially an effective simple against the routine ache of Big D. But then someone communicated to me the concept of planet death. You might be able to get used to the idea of personal extinction if you thought the world went on for ever, with generations of kids sitting back in amazement as your works chattered through on computer printout, and murmuring a mutated 'Stone me'. But when someone in the Science sixth pointed out to me over lunch that the earth was floating inexorably towards a last burn-up, it gave a new look to the robustness of art. LPs syruping; sets of Dickens flaring up at Fahrenheit 451; Donatellos melting like Dali watches. Get out of that one.

Or get out of this one. Suppose, just suppose that someone came up with a cure for death. It wouldn't necessarily be any more improbable than the splitting of the atom or the discovery of radio waves. But it would be a long process, like finding a cure for cancer. And they aren't exactly hurrying along with it at the moment. So you can be pretty sure that if ever they do find a way of delaying death, it'll be just a bit too late for you …

Or get out of this one. Suppose they find a way, even after you are dead, of reconstituting you. What if they dig up your coffin and find you're just a bit too putrefied ... What if you've been cremated and they can't find all the grains ... What if the State Revivification Committee decides you're not important enough ... What if you're in the middle of being brought back to life when some dumb nurse, overcome by the significance of her task, drops a vital phial, and your clearing vision hazes over eternally ... What if ...

Once, foolishly, I asked my brother if he were frightened of death.

'Bit early, isn't it?' He was practical, logical, short-sighted. He was also eighteen and about to go to Leeds University to read economics.

'But don't you ever worry about it? Try and work out what it's all about?'

'It's quite obvious what it's all about, isn't it? Kaput, finito, curtains.' He drew a flattened hand across his throat. 'Anyway, I'm more interested in studying *la petite mort* at the moment.' He grinned, knowing that I wouldn't understand, even though I was meant to be the linguist in the family. I didn't.

I must, however, have jumped at his gesture, because he then drew out of me with a show of sympathy all my personal and cosmic fears. Strangely, they meant nothing to him, even though his entire reading consisted of SF, and he daily absorbed stories about extended life, reincarnation, transubstantiation and the like. My own delicate and appalled imagination couldn't cope with such stuff, neither with the prose nor the ideas. Nigel either had a less touchy imagination, or he had a firmer, less anguished grasp of the termination of his own existence. He seemed to treat the whole of life as a sort of transaction, a deal. It was, he would maintain, a taxi-ride which was good fun, but had to be paid for eventually; a game which would prove pointless without a final whistle; a fruit which, once come to ripeness, had fulfilled its function and must, of necessity, fall from the tree. Easeful, deceptive metaphors, they seemed to me, compared to a vision of infinitely receding blackness.

Nigel's discovery of my fears brought him sharp pleasure.

Every so often, he would look up from his copy of *New SF* or *Asteroids* or *Worlds Beyond* and with a serious expression encourage me to

'Keep going, kid. Last out till 2057 and you'll be able to check in for Body Renewal.' Or Time Transfer, or Molecular Stabilisation, or Brain Banking, or any of a dozen phrases which, I suspect, he made up to tease me with. I never bothered to check in his mags; there may, after all, have been a tiny percentage of truth in it; or if not that, then something different to start my fears and my imagination.

I often wondered about Nigel, and why things seemed so much clearer to him. Was it more, or less, intelligence; more, or less, imagination; or simply a more stable personality? Was it merely perhaps a question of time and energy: that the more industrious you were (and he was always doing something, even if it was only reading pulp), the less broody you got?

When doubts stirred in me, Mary at least could be relied upon to make me feel better. She was always a comforting shambles. My favourite memory of my sister was of her kneeling on the floor bawling, with one of her pigtails neatly plaited and the other undone: the rubber band had broken and there were no more left in the house. She had been faced with the harrowing choice between ribbons, which she hated as cissy, and using the remaining band on a single, central plait.

Her crying jags were a constant feature of my childhood. The dog had a thorn in its paw, she didn't understand the subjunctive, a friend of hers at school knew someone whose aunt had been slightly hurt in a road accident, the retail price index was rising – everything would set her off. Good for morale though it was to have her bawling, it was a noisy way to feel better. Once, I made the mistake of asking her what she thought happened after death. She looked up with that help-me, pleading, blubby look in her eye. I didn't give her time to flee the room. I ran myself.

10 · *Tunnels, Bridges*

Life at sixteen was wonderfully enclosed and balanced. On one side, there was the compulsion of school, hated and enjoyed. On the other side, the compulsion of home, hated and enjoyed. Out there, vague and marvellous as the Empyrean, lay capital-L Life. There were sometimes things – like holidays – which seemed as if they might give a foretaste of life; yet they always turned out to count as home after all.

But there was a point of balance in the oscillation between home and school. The journey. An hour and a quarter each way, a time of twice-daily metamorphosis. At one end, on the whole, you appeared clean, tidy, hard-working, conservative, responsibly questioning, unworried by sex, attracted by a fair division of life between work and play, not unhealthily interested in art: a pride, if usually less than a joy, to your parents. At the other end, you slouched out of the carriage, shoes scuffed, tie askew, nails neurotically bitten, palms forested by wanking, satchel held in front of you to conceal an expiring hard, loud-mouthed with *merde* and bugger and balls and fug (our only euphemism), lazy yet smirkingly confident, obsequious and deceitful, contemptuous of authority, mad about art, emotionally homosexual for want of choice, and obsessed with the idea of nudist camps.

Needless to say, you never noticed the transformation yourself. Nor would an outsider have spotted it: at the point of change, he would merely have seen an averagely clean schoolboy, his satchel on his knees, testing himself on French vocabulary with a sheet of paper half-covering the page, and every so often looking up and staring out of the window.

Those daily journeys were, I now realise, the only times when I was safely alone. Perhaps that was why I never found them tiring or boring, despite sitting for years with the same chalk-striped men and watching out of the same window the same scenery and then the same tunnel walls, their sides corrugated with dusty black cables. And every day, of course, there were games to be played which never failed.

The first of these was getting a seat: which was a far from boring business. Frankly, I never cared much where I sat on a train; but I did enjoy sitting where other people wanted to sit. This was the day's first subversive action. Some of the old fuggers who got on at Eastwick actually had favourite places: favourite carriages, favourite sides, a favourite spot in the knotted string rack for their bowlers. Frustrating their contemptible hopes was a fine game, and not too hard, since you weren't forced to play by the adult rules. The pinstripes and the chalkstripes always forced themselves to get their favourite place without appearing to care where they sat, yet casually sticking out their fatty hips and metal-cornered attaché cases in an attempt to grab pole position. As a kid you were obviously a rule-free beast whom self-restraint and the laws of society had not yet forced into not grabbing what you wanted (or actually, in this case, not grabbing what you didn't care whether you had or not). So as you waited for the train you would lurk around uncertainly, changing your place on the platform to put the wind up the old fugs. Then you might make a dash for a door as the train came in; even break all the rules by wrenching a door open before the train had stopped.

The coolest thing of all to do – though it took a lot of nerve – was just to beat some old turd to his favourite seat and then, as you saw him settling resentfully for second-best, get up casually and flop down in some obviously less desirable area of the compartment. Then you stared at him knowingly. Since they rarely owned up to their desires, but clearly knew that you knew them, you won twice.

The tricks of travel were learned early. How to fold a full-size newspaper vertically so that you could turn over in the width of one page. How to pretend you hadn't seen the sort of women you were expected to stand up for. Where to stand in a full train to get the best chance of a seat when it began to empty. Where to get on a train so that you got off at just the right spot. How to use the no-exit tunnels for short-cuts. How to use your season ticket beyond its permitted range.

These preoccupations kept you limbered up. But there were fuller experiences to be had as well.

'Don't you ever get bored?' Toni once asked as we were adding up the months and years of our lives we had spent on trains. He only had a ten-stop ride round the Circle Line: uneventful, all underground, no chance of rape or abduction.

'Nah. Too much going on.'

'Tunnels, bridges, telegraph poles?'

'That sort of thing. No, actually, things like Kilburn. It's Doré; it really is.'

The next half-day, Toni came to try it out. Between Finchley Road and Wembley Park the train goes over a high viaduct system at Kilburn. Below, as far as you could see, lay cross-hatched streets of tall, run-down Victorian terraces. Half a dozen television aerials interwoven on every roof implied a honeycomb of plasterboard partitioning beneath. There were few cars in that sort of area at that time, and no visible greenery. A huge, regular, red-brick Victorian building stood in the middle: a monster school, infirmary, lunatic asylum – I never knew, nor wanted that sort of precision. The value of Kilburn depended on not knowing particularities, because it changed to the eye and the brain according to yourself, your mood and the day. On a late afternoon in winter, with the egg-white lamps faintly beginning to show, it was melancholy and frightening, the haunt of acid-bath murderers. On a clear, bright morning in summer, with almost no smog and lots of people visible, it was like a brave little slum in the Blitz: you half expected to see George VI poking around the few remaining bomb-sites with his umbrella. Kilburn could suggest to you the pullulating mass of the working class, who any moment might swarm like termites up the viaduct and take the pin-stripes apart; equally, it could be a comforting proof that so many people could live together quietly at close quarters.

Toni and I got off at Wembley Park, changed platforms, and went back over the area. Then we did the same again.

'Christ, there're so many of them,' was Toni's eventual comment. Thousands of people down there, all within a few hundred yards of you; yet you'd never, in all probability, meet any of them.

'Well, it's an argument against God, isn't it?'

'Yeah. And for enlightened dictatorship.'

'And for art for art's sake.'

He was silent for a while, awed.

'Well, I take it back, I take it back.'

'Thought you might. There are others, but this is the best.' Toni silently got back on the next Baker Street train for his final run over the stretch.

From then on, I was not only interested in my journey, but proud of it. The termitary of Kilburn; the grimy, lost stations between Baker Street and Finchley Road; the steppe-like playing-fields at Northwick Park; the depot at Neasden, full of idle, aged rolling-stock; the frozen faces of passengers glimpsed in the windows of fast Marylebone trains. They were all, in some way, relevant, fulfilling, sensibility-sharpening. And what was life about if not that?

11 · *SST*

Things never changed for you. That was one of the first rules. You talked about what things would be like when they did change: you imagined marriage, and sex eight times a night, and bringing up your children in a way which combined flexibility, tolerance, creativeness and large quantities of money; you thought of having a bank account and going to strip clubs and owning cufflinks, collar studs and monogrammed handkerchiefs. But any real threat of change induced apprehension and discontent.

For the duration, things changed only for other people. The school swimming master was thrown out for queering up boys in the changing rooms ('ill health', they told us); Holdsworth, an amiable thug in 5B, was expelled for pouring sugar into the petrol tank of a master's Humber Super Snipe; the children of neighbours did amazing, incredible things, like joining Shell and being posted abroad, or souping up bangers, or going to dances on New Year's Eve. The house equivalent of such disturbances was that my brother got a girl friend.

Psychic blows normally come from other directions, don't they? Like a son growing taller than his father, a daughter's tits bursting out beyond her mother's marginal convexities, siblings fancying one another? Or from jealousy – about possessions, about lack of spots, about academic success. There was very little of this in our family: our father was taller and stronger than both his sons; Mary evoked compassion rather than lust; and all three of us children had an equitable handout of goods and facial bad luck.

In fact, when my brother got a girl friend, it wasn't really jealousy I felt. It was straight fear, quickened with a little hate. Nigel brought her home the first time without any proper warning from the Front Seat. Suddenly, half an hour before dinner, there was this girl in among us – shiny sort of dress, handbag, hair, eyes, lipstick; just like a woman in fact. And with my brother! Tits? I asked myself in furtive panic. Well, you couldn't really see, not with that dress. But even so, a girl! My eyes stood out like chapel hatpegs. I knew, too, that I could rely on Nigel not to miss my fearful response.

'Ginny, this is my father,' (our mother was slaving in the kitchen to produce 'just an ordinary supper') 'and this is my little sis, Mary. This is the dog; this is the telly; this is the fire-place. Oh, and this,' (turning to the chair in which I was sitting) 'is the chair in which you're going to be sitting.'

I got up, sheepish and enraged, having a go at smiling.

'Oh, sorry, kid, didn't see you. This is Chris; Chris Baude-laire – he's adopted. He doesn't stand up when he meets girls, but that's probably just an attack of spleen.'

I stuck out a hand and tried to make up for lost ground.

'What did you say her name was, this chippy of yours?' I asked; but somehow it didn't come out as witty and ironic; just gawky and ill-bred.

'Jeanne Duval to you,' he replied, despite warning glances from our father. 'And next time, Chris, you don't put out the hand until it's offered, OK?'

I sat back in my chair again, as an act of aggression. Nigel sat 'her' on the sofa next to him. Then they both got the sherry treatment. I stared at the girl's legs, but couldn't find any fault. Not knowing what to look for didn't help. Her stockings seemed all right too – no holes, seams straight, and despite a low sofa tipping her backwards, there wasn't a touch of stocking top (which I yearned for, and yearned to disapprove of).

I spent the whole evening hating Ginny (what a stupid

name for a start). Hating her for what she was doing to my brother (like helping him grow up); hating her for what she was going to do to my relationship with him (like ending the few boyish games we still played together); and hating her, most of all, for being herself. A girl, a different order of being.

The evening was full of humiliating reminders that I was still a kid. I didn't get wine with my dinner (I didn't like wine, but that was hardly the point) and my glass of orange squash mocked me unbearably. I tried ignoring it at first, but found it grew louder and more contemptuous in colour as the meal progressed, until, by the time the matching orange pudding was brought in, it was practically flashing out I-M-M-A-T-U-R-E like an illuminated sign, and I gulped it down in one draught. My attempts to assert bonds of adolescence with my brother went unanswered; my appeals to holidays, shared japes, my God even SF, were all rebuffed. The culminating moment came when I turned to Nigel and began

'Do you remember when we ... '

but got no further as he broke in with a forcefully languid

'Can't say I do, kid.'

At which this girl, this Ginny, simpered. Christ, she was obnoxious. I scarcely looked at her all evening; I certainly didn't listen to the little she said; enough that I hated her. She simpered, she pouted, she played up to the Front Seat, she made hypocritical noises about the food. Wait till I told Toni about *her*. We'd mince *her*.

'My brother brought his new chippy home last night,' I told Toni casually, as we sipped our milk during break the next morning with the habitual, affected disgust of gourmets (you never knew, there might be someone watching). He frowned his eyebrows together and twinkled his eyes. Here came the SST test.

'Soul?'

'No, absolutely none, I'd say. No more than most, if you ask me. Still waters running shallow is what it looked like.'

'Suffering?'

'Well, her father's dead, I managed to get that out of her,

but when I started asking if it was suicide they all pretended to be fantastically épated and shut me up. She toadied like a hot bitch to my mum, which may of course mean that her own beat her as a kid.'

'Yeah, or it may just mean she wanted to grease up.'

'She's certainly got some Two-S coming to her though.'

'How?'

'Going around with my bro.'

'Do you think he's tried it on?'

'She sat next to him on the sofa.'

'Collar test? Hair test? Eye interchange?'

'All negative. We didn't have the telly on, unfortunately. I tried to push for *Wells Fargo*, but no one seemed keen.'

Toni and I had worked out an infallible television test. No one can watch a kiss – at least, a long-drawn-out oil-drilling sort of kiss – without somehow giving away what they feel. You couldn't observe directly, but by sitting close to the telly and staring at the reflection in the screen, you could usually spot coarse reactions: my brother crossing his legs, my mother jumpily deciding to count the stitches in her knitting. If you wanted a finer focus, you had to rely on dangerous tricks, like leaping up to get a glass of orange, or reaching across for the *Radio Times*. Then, briefly, as you turned, you might catch heaving nostalgia (my father), embarrassed boredom (my mother), technical interest (Nigel), or querulous puzzlement (Mary). Visitors were equally transparent, despite away manners.

'Tits?'

The final part of the triad, the part to which we brought all our worldly perceptiveness.

'Didn't see hide nor hair. Perhaps – and I'm being generous – a couple of verrucas.'

'Ah.' Toni relaxed his eyebrows, satisfied and relieved. He hadn't missed anything after all.

12 · Hard and Low

Toni and I spent a hefty amount of time together being bored. Not bored with each other, of course – we were at that irrecoverable age when friends can be hateful, irritating, disloyal, stupid or mean, but can never be boring. Adults were boring, with their rationality, their deference, their refusal to punish you as severely as you knew you ought to be punished. Adults were useful because they were boring: they were raw material; they were predictable in their responses. They might be wet and kindly, or sour and vicious; but they were always predictable. They made you believe in advance in the integrity of character.

'What shall we be today?' Toni and I would sometimes ask each other. It was a direct denial of adult status. Adults were always themselves. We, by popular insistence, were not yet grown up, not yet formed; no one knew how we would 'turn out'. We could, at least, make a few trial gestures on our own account.

'How are you going to turn out?'

'Like a jelly?'

'Like a light?'

'Like a Sandhurst cadet?'

We hadn't yet turned out. Being protean was our only consistent shape. Everything was justifiable. Everything was possible.

'What shall we be today?'

'Why don't we be supporters of the Firsts?'

It was a seductive idea. We were always searching for new pockets of character within ourselves; and it was always enjoyable to try something finely alien. The Head was continually appealing for boys to waste their valuable Saturday afternoons by going to support the First XV; especially at away matches, when the pressure of six or eight parents from the opposite side baying for victory, plus the disorientation of a train journey to an unfamiliar ground, were always good enough to buckle the morale of our insecure team. On this occasion, Toni and I headed off to watch the school play Merchant Taylors, whose ground was a mere ten minutes' bike ride from Eastwick.

'How shall we do it,' I asked, 'straight or clever?'

'We couldn't be too clever in case Telford reports us.'

'True.'

'Mustn't be too straight, though.'

'No fear.'

Telford was the brute who ran the First XV, a tyrant in a trench mackintosh who drove a Singer Vogue to away games, and whose tireless exhortations of 'Feet, School, feeeeEEEEt' would wail across the frostbound pitch from the opposite touchline.

'Have to stay away from the side Telltale's on.'

'Yeah. I think we'd better do it completely straight at first, only fantastically enthusiastically – up and down the touch, waving our scarves, shouting out the score just in case they forget it. Then, as they begin to lose, we carry on in exactly the same way, so that it gradually becomes more and more piss-taking, only Telltale won't be able to get us for it.'

It sounded a foolproof scheme. We stationed ourselves on the less tenanted touchline and roared and cheered while School fumbled, missed tackles, dropped the ball, got offside, passed the ball forward while inches from the line, and wheeled their scrum in opposite directions at the same time.

'Bad luck, School.'

'Keep plugging away, School.'

'Hard and low, man, hard and low.'

'Drive, School, drive. On, on, on. Feet, feet, feet. Oh, tough luck, School. Now's your chance to get one back.'

'Only thirty points, School. Wind in your backs second half!'

'Fall, fall. Die with it!'

This last was the meanest cry available. Whenever the ball went loose, and a frail, tentative inside centre was pretending to wait for it to stop bouncing, but was really keeping a wary eye on the advancing posse of enemy forwards, we would let rip. If the man didn't fall on the ball, he was manifestly a coward. If he picked it up and booted for touch before the enemy scragged him, he was still manifestly a coward. If he fell on it, the chances were that the primitive techniques of rucking which obtained in schools rugby would leave him quite satisfactorily maimed. Best of all was to get him to fall unnecessarily early, watch him lie there until fully trampled, and then have the ref award a penalty for failing to release the ball on the ground.

As the match wore on, as the following wind made all School's passes drift forward, the enemy lazily doubled their lead. Toni and I reflected on the pity that School didn't have anyone of the calibre of Camus or Henri de in their pack. Gradually, we noticed that our men were beginning to play to the other touchline. Kicks, even from our side of the pitch, were invariably directed to the more difficult touch; passing movements went that way too. Once, when a rare piece of blind-side action took place close to where we stood, the School scrum half (Fisher, N. J. – not a person of cultivation) chose to ignore an overlap and booted the ball at Toni and me from a few feet away; it passed between us at ruination-level and carried on for thirty yards or so. Toni and I somehow didn't offer to run and collect it; instead we stood there, five yards from the steaming line-out, offering vigorous and well-thought-out advice.

'Run it, School.'

'No point kicking at this stage.'

'Time to really put on the pressure.'

'Final rally. Full eighty minutes, School.'

'Jump!'

'Bad luck, School. Now hard in there, *hard*.'

'Now make this *yours*.'

'Hard and low, hard and low.'

'Fall, fall, fall. Die with it.'

Wisely, we thought we'd probably seen the best of the match when there were still five minutes to go; with a final 'On, on, School', we scrammed. It would be two days before we saw any of that lot again.

As we bicycled home, the evening thickened enthusiastically; bits of fog began to loiter hopefully by the laurel hedges. Along the Rickmansworth Road, every third street-lamp flickered and flashed into life. Passing through each patch of orange light, we avoided looking at each other; it was bad enough seeing your own brown fingers on the handlebars.

'Do you think,' Toni mused, 'we could call that an épat?'

'Well, they were certainly all dead bourgeois, that's for sure. Do you think they knew we were fugging around with them, though?'

'I think they might have done.'

'Yeah, me too.' I was always keen to claim as many épats as possible. Toni, on the other hand, tended to be a bit pernickety.

'But I think it might be presuming a bit much to think that they'll reflect for very long on what we were trying to teach them about the games ethic.'

'Isn't it still an épat even if they don't hoist it in?'

'I don't know.'

'Nor do I.'

We cycled on; now, two in every three lamps were casting their unreal light.

'What will become of them all?'

'Poor fuggers. Bank managers, I suppose.'

'They can't all become bank managers.'

'I don't know about that. There's nothing to say they can't.'

'No; true.' Toni became quite excited. 'Hey, what about that? What about if the *whole school*, apart from us, became bank managers. Wouldn't that be great?'

It would be terrific. It would be perfect.

'And how do you see us?' I usually deferred to Toni on matters of the future.

'I see us,' he replied, 'as artists-in-residence at a nudist colony.'

That too would be terrific; perfect.

We cycled back to Eastwick. Ahead lay more discussions; then, the blindfolds, and on with ('Clear water; Hampton Court maze?; shoulders wanting to swing; chirpiness – bit as if you've just had a blood transfusion. Stuttgart CO/Münchinger') Bach.

13 · Object Relations

Things.

How does adolescence come back most vividly to you? What do you remember first? The quality of your parents; a girl; your first sexual tremor; success or failure at school; some still unconfessed humiliation; happiness; unhappiness; or, perhaps, a trivial action which first revealed to you what you might later become? I remember things.

When I look back, I always seem to be sitting up in bed at the day's end; too sleepy to read, yet too awake to put off the light and face the tentacular fears of the night.

The walls of my bedroom are ash grey, a colour appropriate to the local *Weltanschauung*. To my left is my bookcase, each paperback (Rimbaud and Baudelaire within reach) lovingly covered in transparent Fablon. My name is written in each one, on the top edge of the inside front cover, so that the Fablon, folded over to a depth of half an inch, covers the decisive capitals of CHRISTOPHER LLOYD. This device prevents erasure and, in theory, theft.

Next, my dressing-table. A crocheted mat; two hairbrushes so stuffed with hair that I have abandoned them and taken to a comb; clean socks and white shirt for the morning; a blue plastic knight, made up from a model kit given me by Nigel one Christmas, and left half-painted; finally, a small musical box which I play continually even though I don't like its dreary Swiss tune – I just play it for the weary, grinding way it behaves when the power begins to run out and the spiked drum strains to flick the metal fingers.

A grey wall, with a curling poster of Monet's greyest version of Rouen Cathedral. My Dansette record player, with a few experimental discs beside it.

To my right, a wardrobe, lockable but never locked. At the bottom of it is a deliberate pile of papers, holiday hats, deflated beach balls, discarded jeans and secondhand box-files, all heaped up to hide a few precious things (a copy of *Reveille*, a letter or two from Toni) which I hope won't be discovered. Also in the wardrobe, my two school jackets, my best greys, my second-best greys, my third-best greys, my cricket trousers. When I shut the door, half a dozen metal hangers tinkle to remind me of clothes I don't have. The whole room is full of things I don't have.

Next, a chair draped with the day's dumped clothes. Propped against it is a suitcase on which, every so often, I mentally stick labels. The labels indicate several generations of travel; some are grubby and tattered; all imply *l'adieu suprême des mouchoirs*. I can go; I will go. So far the case is label-less: it is all to come. One day I shall fix the real labels on myself. It is all to come.

Last, my bedside table, containing the only object which has actually come from abroad – the bedside lamp. A fat wine flask wrapped in plastic cane, it was brought back from some Portuguese resort by a roving cousin, and has devolved to me from my sister; it upset her. My watch, which I despise because it doesn't have a second hand. A Fablon-covered book.

Objects redolent of all I felt and hoped for; yet objects which I myself had only half-willed, only half-planned. Some I chose, some were chosen for me, some I consented to. Is that so strange? What else are you at that age but a creature part willing, part consenting, part being chosen?

PART TWO
Paris (1968)

Moi qui ai connu Rimbaud, je sais
qu'il se foutait pas mal si A
était rouge ou vert. Il le voyait
comme ça, mais c'est tout.

Verlaine to Pierre Louÿs

'So you lived in Paris for a while?'

'Yuh.'

'When was that?'

I never actually lie, though for a time I used to try and discourage the obvious follow-ups. I would never mention May for a start. Early summer was the nearest I'd admit to.

'Nineteen … ' (a frown of bad memory; mouth like a fish's searching on the surface) ' … must have been sixty-eight.'

Increasingly, though, the year has little effect, and I no longer feel it's cheating to start blurring my dates. 'Oh, late Sixties.' 'Sixty-seven, eight, round about then.' For a few years, however, I used to have to dodge out of the way of a variety of replies.

'Oh, what, when those awful … ' friends of my parents would begin, eyeing me palely and filling my pockets with cobblestones.

'Did you see anything of … ' was the usual, mid-way response, as if we were running through films seen, or mutual friends.

And then there was a third type of follow-up, the cool one I felt most uneasy with.

'Ah,' (a shift in the chair, a tapping of the pipe, or some other settling social gesture) '*les événements.*' It wouldn't have been so bad if it had been put as a question. But it would always be a statement; then there would be a respectful, rallying pause, disturbed only, say, by the creak of an unbroken leather jacket. If I failed to leap into the silence, there would (with the kindly assumption that I was suffering from shellshock) be a helpful supplementary:

'I knew a guy out there at the time ... ' or

'Now what I've always found unclear ... ' or

'Right on ... '

The point is – well I was there, all through May, through the burning of the Bourse, the occupation of the Odéon, the Billancourt lock-in, the rumours of tanks roaring back through the night from Germany. But I didn't actually see anything. I can't, to be honest, remember even a smudge of smoke in the sky. Where did they put up all their posters? Not where I was living. Neither can I remember the newspaper headlines of the time; I suppose the papers went on as usual – I might have remembered if they'd stopped. Louis XVI (if you'll forgive the comparison) went out hunting on the day the Bastille fell, came home and wrote in his diary that evening, '*Rien*'. I came home and wrote for weeks on end, 'Annick'. Not just that, of course: her name would be followed by paragraphs of hoarse delight, wry self-congratulation, and feigned moping; but was there any room in that panting, exultant journal for any 'sharp vignettes of the struggle', for any lumbering political reflections? I haven't kept the diary, but I can't believe there was.

Recently, Toni showed me a letter I'd written him from Paris, which contained a rare comment on the crisis. My explanation of the troubles, it seems, was that the students were too stupid to understand their courses, became mentally frustrated, and because of the lack of sports facilities had taken to fighting the riot police. 'You may have seen a rather well-structured photograph', I wrote, 'of a group of police chasing a student into the river. The student is turning sideways towards the camera. A touch of Lartigue about it. At least he got some exercise. *Mens seina in corpore seino.*'

Toni still occasionally quotes me phrases from that letter when he thinks I'm getting complacent; which is most of the time. Apparently, the student involved was drowned – or at least that's what some people said – though even if it were true,

I wasn't to know at the time, was I? Toni, naturally enough, is fairly scathing about my whole Parisian experience.

'Absolutely fucking typical. Only time you've been in the right place at the right time in your whole life, I'd say, and where are you? Holed up in an attic stuffing some chippy. It almost makes me believe in cosmic order, it's so appropriate. I suppose you were mending your bike during that skirmish of 14–18? Doing your eleven-plus during Suez?' (Actually, yes, more or less) 'And what about the Trojan wars?'

'On the lav.'

1 · Karezza

At twenty-one, I used to say I believed in the deferment of pleasure; I was usually misunderstood. Deferment was the word, not rejection or repression or abandonment or all the other terms it automatically got translated into. I'm less sure now, though I do believe in the balanced, delicate leading-in of the individual to experience. This isn't prescriptive; just sensible. How many kids of twenty-one today are sentiently burnt out; or worse, find it chic to believe they are? Isn't a diet of extremity senseless and, finally, comic? Isn't the whole structure of experience built on contrast?

What I'm leading up to is that when I arrived in Paris, with almost two decades of education behind me, plus an enthralled reading in the classics of passion – Racine, Marivaux, Laclos were trusted guides – I was still a virgin. Now, don't jump to all those conclusions (puritanism lurking behind stance of worldly knowledge; fear of sex disguised as austerity; sneaky jealousy of today's kids) because I know them already. The fact that pubescents nowadays are getting stuck in before their testicles are fully descended doesn't bother me in itself. Not really. Not very often.

'Maybe you just don't like sex?' Toni would whisper at me, after what we called the Common Pursuit had led, in his case, to joining the Great Tradition. 'Time to Revalue, kid,' he commanded.

'I know I like it – that's why I can refuse it.' I liked this argument.

'You can't mean you know you like it; you mean you think you will like it.'

'All right.' If he wanted to put it that way. 'Anyway, De Rougemont says passion thrives on obstacles.'

'That doesn't mean you have to build your own. Do It Yourself artist. Why don't you want to get in there and root? Root de toot. I mean, Christ, I want to root everyone.' Toni made a few rolling, nasal pig-noises. 'I can barely think of a woman I *don't* want to fuck. Think of all that pussy out there, Chris; all that dripping fur. You're not exactly a warpie. It's true you don't seem to have the tremendous drive that I've got' (Toni, admittedly, did look older, more rabbit-hungry) 'but I should think most women, given the opportunity, would go down on you like a ton of bricks. I mean, knock out those over seventy, no fifty, and those under fifteen, nuns, religious screw-ups, most newly marrieds but not all, a few million with malnutrition whom you probably wouldn't want to touch, your mother, your sister, no on second thoughts we may as well leave her in you never know, your gran, plus June Ritchie and anyone I happen to be going around with at the time – and what have we got? Hundreds of millions of women all of whom mightn't be averse to breaking in the old dick. French, Italians, *Swedes*,' (he cocked an eyebrow) 'Americans, Persians ... ?' (he put his head on one side) 'Japanese – the inscrutable yoni? *Malaysians*? Creoles? Eskimos? Burmese?' (an impatient shrug) 'Red Indians? Latvians? *Irish*?' (then, crossly) 'Zulus?' He paused, a shopkeeper who has spread out his best stuff and knows that if you only address your mind to the matter, you'll find something you like.

'I didn't realise you wanked over the atlas.'

'Graduated from the *National Geographic*.'

'Well, who didn't?'

'But you could have by now, couldn't you?' (Toni, like a dutiful air-traffic controller, was always monitoring what he called my 'near misses') 'There was that nurse, wasn't there, who said if you were good, the next time you could have chocolates?'

'Yes.'

'And that girl who wasn't Jewish, wasn't Catholic and had been to X-films?'

'Yes.'

'And that woman when you were on the Christmas post?'

'I might have lost my bonus.'

'That's what it's all about, kid, losing your bonus. And Rusty, for fuck's sake, Rusty ... '

Rusty was actually Janet, but Toni had given her a pulp sobriquet partly, I think, because of his tendency to Americanise sex; but officially because, he claimed, he was afraid that if I didn't finally hurl one past her (as he, not I, would have put it), she might rust up.

After leaving school, I'd spent a couple of months knocking around with Rusty. She was the local solicitor's daughter and fulfilled our SST qualifications. (Though in her case, it was more like TSS. She had big tits and was unhappy. Toni deduced with impregnable logic that she was unhappy because, as soon as her tits became larger than her mother's, her parents gave her a hard time; so she had Suffered; and if you had Suffered, you couldn't not have Soul.) Janet and I used to lie around in the sun, which I almost enjoyed (though I suspected I would always be oppidan at heart: my cool soul needed to be indoors, like a stick of rhubarb growing best in an upturned chimney-pot). We went for walks and laughed at golfers; we tried learning to smoke; we thought about the capital-F Future. I explained that I was part of the Anger Generation; she asked me if this meant I wasn't going to take a job; I said I wasn't sure – you could never tell which way Anger was going to jump; she said she understood.

Janet/Rusty was the first girl with whom I exchanged kisses of respectable duration; the first, that is, with whom I realised that you were only allowed to breathe through your nose. Initially, it was like being at the dentist's: you spent all the time hoping that your one operative air-passage wouldn't clog up before you got out of the chair. Gradually, though, I got my confidence. After that, it felt more like snorkelling.

I snorkelled a lot with Janet. She was almost the love of part of my life.

'She was almost the love of part of my life.'

'You said.'

'Does it still sound OK?'

'Yeah, it's OK – wry, if thin-blooded; but I suppose that's about right. So why didn't you ever shoot one past Rusty?'

'Why are your metaphors always taken from sport? Scoring, shooting, hurling, hitting a home run. Why do you make it sound so competitive?'

'Because it is, it is. And if you don't look out, you'll get relegated. Rusty, I mean, Rusty … ' He did a lost-for-lust face and waved his hands around like a black-and-white minstrel.

'Did you fancy her then?'

'Fancy her? If it hadn't been for you, I'd … '

' … 've scored five goals, three boundaries, two knock-outs, eight home runs and broken the marathon record while you were about it.'

'Pole vault.'

'Javelin.'

'Shot putt.' He pretended to juggle two monster breasts in his weighed-down palms.

'Hop, step and thump.'

'Why not, Chris?'

'Just because you can, it doesn't mean you have to.'

'If you can, and you want to, then you ought to.'

'If you do just because you ought to, then you don't really want to.'

'If you can, and you want to, and you don't, then you're queer.'

'It was the man in Rusty I loved.'

Rusty/Janet and I spent quite some time not undressing each other. Partly it was lack of opportunity, although – as I would argue grandly to myself – the ingenious and the desperate always find some sodden undergrowth, some disc-slipping back seat, or nervous shop doorway flicker-lit by passing cars. But then, I suppose we weren't desperate, and our ingenuity was limited to making our parents believe that we didn't really mind whether we were left alone or not; that way, we were left alone more.

Sometimes, though, we'd go in for a playful, partial, half-amused investigation of each other. We'd expose a small area of the other's body – a crescent of breast, a band of belly, a shoulder, a thigh. On the few occasions we undressed totally, there was a sense of let-down afterwards. But it wasn't, I came to realise later, the sense of frustration at not making love; it was a vaguer feeling, the sort of dissatisfaction you get when you've achieved something rather than the sort you get when you've failed. I wondered whether the pleasure of striving didn't exceed the pleasure of achievement, of victory, of orgasm. Maybe the ultimate in sexual fulfilment would prove to be *karezza*? It is, I used to tell Toni from the sanctuary of virginity, only our competitive, games-playing society which makes us head noisily for the white tape of orgasm.

2 · Demandez Nuts

Still, I don't know how important all that stuff is.

Paris. 1968. Annick. A delightful Breton name, isn't it? The -ick, by the way, is pronounced with a long i, to rhyme with pique, which isn't appropriate, at least not at first.

I'd gone to Paris to do some research for part of a thesis I'd undertaken so that I could get a grant and go to Paris. A completely normal sense of priorities among post-graduates. At the time, friends of mine were loafing their way – constructively or otherwise – through most of the capital cities of Europe, after developing furious interests in matters which could only be thoroughly investigated where the relevant papers happened to be. In my case, it was 'The Importance and Influence of British Styles of Acting in the Paris Theatre 1789–1850'. You always need to shove at least one big date (1789, 1848, 1914) into your title, because it looks more efficient, and flatters the general belief that everything changes with the eruption of war. Actually, as I rapidly discovered, things do change: thus, in the years immediately after 1789, the British Styles of Acting had very little Importance and Influence in the Paris Theatre, for the simple reason that no British actor in his right mind would have risked his skin over there while the Revolution was on. I suppose I should have guessed this. But to tell the truth, the only thing I knew about British acting in France when I invented the subject was that Berlioz fell in love with Harriet Smithson in 1827. She, of course, as it turned out, was Irish; but then I was only applying for money for six months in Paris, and the financial authorities weren't an over-sophisticated bunch.

'*Can-can, frou-frou, vin blanc,* French knickers,' was Toni's comment when I told him I was off to Paris. He was going to Morocco for his de-Anglification, and was already racking up spoolfuls of tortured hisses and grunts on his Grundig.

'Kif. Hashish. Lawrence of Arabia. Dates,' was my reply, though I felt it lacked a certain edge.

But it wasn't really like that. I'd already been to Paris many times before 1968, and didn't go with any of the naïve expect-ations Toni was greedy to attribute to me. I'd already done the Paree side of it in my late teens: green Olympia Press paper-backs, ocular loitering from boulevard cafés, thrusting leather G-strings and pouches in a Montparnasse simulation-dive. I'd done the city-as-history bit while a student, I-spying the famous in Père Lachaise, and coming back exultant over an un-expected find: the catacombs at Denfer-Rochereau, where post-Revolutionary history and personal glooming could be sweetly combined as you wandered among vaults of trans-planted skeletons, sorted and stacked by bone rather than body: neat banks of femurs and solid cubes of skulls suddenly rose up before the groping light of your candle. I'd even, by this time, stopped sneering at my exhausted compatriots who clogged the cafés round the Gare du Nord, waving fingers to indicate the number of Pernods they wanted.

I chose Paris because it was a familiar place where I could, if I wanted to, live alone. I knew the city; I knew the language; I wouldn't be harassed by the food or the climate. It was too large to have a menacingly hospitable colony of English émigrés. There would be little to stop me concentrating on myself.

I was lent a flat up in Buttes-Chaumont (the clanking 7-*bis* Métro line: Bolivar, Buttes-Chaumont, Botzaris) by a friend-of-a-friend. It was an airy, slightly derelict studio-bedroom with a creaky French floor and a fruit machine in the corner which worked off a supply of old francs kept on a shelf. In the kitchen was a rack of home-made calvados which I was allowed to drink provided I replaced each bottle with a substitute one of whisky (I lost money on the deal, but gained local colour).

I installed my few possessions, greased up to the concierge, Mme Huet, in her den of house-plants and diarrhoeic cats and back numbers of *France Dimanche* (she tipped me off about each *nouvelle intervention chirurgicale à Windsor*), registered at the Bibliothèque Nationale (which wasn't too conveniently close) and began to fancy myself, at long last, as an autonomous being. School, home, university, friends – all in their different ways offered a consensus of values, ambitions, approved styles of failure. You accepted bits, you reacted against bits, you reacted against reacting against bits, and the constant swaying motion of this process gave you the illusion of advance. Here, at last, though, I could really work it out. I'd take a breather and really work it all out.

Well, perhaps not straight away. Just to come here, sit down, and start methodically working out your life: wouldn't that be succumbing to exactly the sort of channelled, Civil Service thinking which I had heroically scorned? So for the first few weeks I loafed, without much trouble or guilt. I called in on the Howard Hawks season which is always playing somewhere in Paris. I sat around knowingly in some of the less celebrated squares and gardens. I rediscovered that smirk which goes with riding first class on a second-class Métro ticket. I looked up a few reports of Revolutionary performances of Addison's *Cato* (the play was a favourite of Marat's). I leafed through accounts of Being Artistic in Paris. I lounged about at Shakespeare & Company. I read Hemingway's posthumous Paris memoirs, rumoured to have been written by his wife ('Out of the question,' Toni had assured me, 'they're so badly written they must be authentic').

I did some rather delicate drawings according to the Haphazard Principle. The theory was that everything is intrinsically interesting, that art shouldn't just concentrate on high-spots (I know *some* people have taken that line before). So you carry your sketch-book everywhere, and stop not according to the official, received interestingness of what you see, but according to some random factor which you decide on that day – like being jostled in the street, or seeing two bicycles abreast, or smelling coffee. Then you freeze, stay pointing in the direction you were heading, and examine the first thing your eye falls on. In a way, it's a development of the old theory Toni and I had called the Constructive Loaf.

I also dabbled in a little writing. Dabbled, that is, with sober enthusiasm. Memory tests, for example, like describing the horse-butcher I patronised once a week (always – I confess to the parody – every Friday) but whom I'd never really looked at until I tried to describe him and realised how much I was missing. Another exercise was to sit at an open window and simply write down what you saw; next day you checked on the selectivity of your vision. Then a few stylistic exercises, inspired by Queneau, intended as knuckle-looseners. And lots of letters, some of them (to my parents) describing what I wasn't doing, and the longer, more cutely phrased ones to Toni describing what I was.

It was a very pleasant existence. Naturally, Toni (who had lasted three weeks in Africa and was now starting work as a WEA lecturer) wrote to rebuke me for its economic unreality. I argued in reply that happiness depended necessarily on the unreality of one plane of your life: that in one area (emotional, financial, professional) you should be living beyond your resources. Hadn't Toni and I laid it down at school?

> Horses for courses
> Husband your forces
> Too few resources
> Ends in divorces.

And then, after a month in Paris, I met Annick. Shouldn't this have added further unreality, further living beyond resources, further happiness? But did it? What was it, that old school adage? Two plusses make a minus?

I met her, I always smile to recall, as a result of one of my rare visits to the Bibliothèque Nationale. I'd put in almost a whole hour there, skimming through some early Victor Hugo letters to see if he had anything to say about English acting while he was working on *Cromwell* (he did and he didn't, if you really want to know – just the odd biassed phrase or two); exhausted by the sight of mass scholarship in action, I'd knocked off early for a quick *vin blanc cassis* at a bar in the Rue de Richelieu which usually competed with the library for my presence. This wasn't inappropriate: the atmosphere here was strongly reminiscent of the Bib Nat itself. The same soporific, businesslike attention to what was in front of you; the quiet shaking of newspapers instead of book pages; the sagely nodding heads; the professional sleepers. Only the espresso machine, snorting like a steam engine, insisted on where you were.

My eye drifted round the comforting visual clichés of the place: the framed law against public drunkenness; the stainless steel counter; the food list offering an austere choice between *sandwich* and *croque*; the wall of libelling mirrors; the murdered-tree hat rack hidden behind the door; the dusty plastic plants up on a high shelf. This time, though, my eye suddenly alighted on

'*Mountolive!*'

There it lay, on the plastic wicker seat of a chair at the next table. The *Livre de Poche* edition, with a bookmark far enough into it to indicate at least doggedness, and probably enthusiasm.

She turned as I spoke. I suddenly thought, 'Christ I don't normally do this,' and my eyes went out of focus as if dissociating themselves from my voice. I'll have to say something.

'You're reading *Mountolive*?' I managed to croak in the local *patois*, and the strain of this modest cerebration persuaded my eyes back into line. She was ...

'As you see.'

(Quick, quick, think of something.)

'Have you read the others?' She had sort of dark hair and ...

'I have read the first two. Naturally, I haven't read *Clea* yet.' Of course not, pretty dumb question, her skin was rather sallow, but unblemished, of course that's often the case, it's only fair skins which get ...

'Oh, naturally. Are you enjoying it?' Why did I keep asking these fucking obvious questions? Of course she was, or she wouldn't have read two and a half books. Why didn't I show I'd read it, tell her that I adored the *Quartet*, that I'd read everything Durrell wrote which I could get my hands on, that I even knew someone who wrote Pursewarden poems.

'Yes, very much, though I don't understand why this one is written more simply and more conventionally than the other two.' Her clothes were grey and black, though that didn't make her look dowdy at all, no she was smart, colours didn't really register so much as the overall ...

'I agree. I mean, I also don't know. Would you like another coffee my name's Christopher Lloyd.' What'll she say? Is she wearing an engagement ring? Does it matter if she says no? Does *Merci* mean Yes thank you or No thank you, shit I can't remember.

'Yes.'

Ah. A breather at last. A minute or two at the bar. No, don't hurry, Gaspard, or whatever your name is, serve everybody else first. Hey, there must be lots of people out in the street who need serving before me. No, actually, come to think of it, better serve me now – she might think I'm one of those people who are so polite they never actually get a drink in theatre intervals. But what shall I have, better not have another of the same, it's only 5.30. Can't change to sophisticated spirits or she'll think me a potential *clochard*, what about a beer, don't really want one, oh well, hope it doesn't seem too grovelling,

'*Deux express, s'il vous plaît.*'

Carrying the coffees back, I concentrated on trying not to spill them. At the same time I concentrated on appearing not to be concentrating. All right, she was sitting with her back to the bar, but there may have been a sly mirror around; and in any case, you have to get the style right from the start – cool without being bourgeois, carefree without being sloppy. One of the coffees spilled over. Quick, which – give it her on grounds of equality, and to see how she handles it, or keep it for myself on grounds of chivalry and risk blowing the whole thing?

Juggling this in my mind, I managed to spill the other coffee.

'Sorry, they're a bit full.'

'That's all right.'

'Sugar?'

'No thanks. You've changed drink?'

'Er yes. I didn't want you to think I was a *clo-clo*.'

She smiled. Even I almost smiled. There's nothing like slang for easing initial doubts. It shows (a) sense of humour, (b) lively interest in the relevant foreign lingo, (c) awareness that friendly verbal intimacy can be attained with a Brit, and you aren't going to have to discuss National Characteristics and *le chapeau melon* in a stilted fashion for the rest of the time.

We chatted, smiled, drank our coffee, were averagely amused together, and put out a few feelers. I suggested how interesting it would be to look at the translation of the *Quartet* and gave myself marks for subtlety; she asked how long my research in Paris would take, and I thought, we're not married yet, you know. Questions which mean nothing or a lot more. I was too jumpy to know whether or not I actually liked her; nonchalance and nervousness gripped me alternately, and according to no rational pattern. For instance, I bungled asking her what her name was: the question shot out of my mouth like an uncontrollable lump of food at a point when the conversation called for a follow-up question on Graham Greene's reputation in France. On the other hand, I managed the when-shall-we-meet-again bit quite well, acting genuine, avoiding both *hauteur* and the more likely, more damaging self-abasement.

I met Annick on a Tuesday, and we agreed we might meet at the same bar the following Friday. If she wasn't there (there was some question of a cousin – why do the French always have cousins? The English don't have cousins the way they do), then I would ring her at the number she had given me. I considered ducking the appointment, but eventually decided to let the heart speak, and rolled up. I had, after all, spent three days wondering what it would be like to be married to her.

In fact, I'd thought about Annick so much that I couldn't remember what she looked like. It was like putting layer after layer of *papier mâché* over an object and gradually seeing the original shape disappear. How terrible if I failed to recognise the woman I'd already been married to for three days. A student friend of mine, who shared similar fantasies and nerves, once worked out a good ploy to counter this difficulty: he had a special pair of broken specs which he would twirl ostentatiously in his hand while waiting for the girl. It always seemed to work, he said; and moreover, when the stratagem was confessed to later, it unfailingly drew an affectionate response from the girl. It mustn't be admitted too soon, of course; one shouldn't, he told me, lead with weakness and incompetence, but they're great standbys later, when you need to play them as warmly human characteristics.

However, as I had perfect sight, I couldn't very well use this ploy; I would just have to get there early and use the passionately-engrossed-in-a-book trick. By the afternoon of our rendezvous, I was trembly, two of my best fingernails were wrecked, and my bladder had been filling up all day with the speed of a lavatory cistern. My hair was OK, my clothes, after much self-debate, had been decided on, my underpants were changed (again) after last-minute re-inspection, and I'd chosen the book I wished to be discovered with: Villiers de l'Isle-Adam's *Contes Cruels*. I'd actually read it once before, so that I was well covered in case it turned out that she had too.

All this may sound cynical and calculating; but that wouldn't really be doing me justice. It was, I liked to think (perhaps still do think), more the result of a sensitive desire to please. It was as much a matter of how I imagined she would like me to appear as of how I would like to appear to her.

'*Salut!*'

I jerked my head out of old Villiers, the jerk and the excitement sending my eyes out of focus again. That solved the problem of whether I'd recognise her.

'Oh, er *salut!*' I started to get up as she started to sit down. We both stopped, laughed, and sat down. So that was what she looked like, yes, a little thinner than I'd remembered, and (when she took off her mackintosh) er, yes, they were, um, very nice, not enormous, but somehow ... well, real? Only Soul and Suffering to go. Her hair was that dark brown sort of colour, centre-parted and dropping fairly straight to her shoulders, where it turned up; her eyes were nice, brown and I suppose the usual size and shape, but very lively; her nose was functional. She gesticulated a lot as we talked. I suppose what I liked most about her was the moving parts – her hands and eyes. You watched her talk as well as listened to her.

We talked about the obvious things – my research, her job in a photographic library, Durrell, films, Paris. You usually do, despite fantasies about the instant meshing of minds, the joyful discovery of shared assumptions. We agreed about most things – but then we would, given my craven urge to please. I don't mean I struck myself as spineless; and I did put in some dissent about Bergman's sense of humour (arguing perkily that he had one). But there was a natural decorum to our investigations; the only major shared assumption was that we should not dislike each other.

After a couple of drinks, we fell on the idea of a film. You can't just go on talking, after all; best to lay down a little shared experience as soon as possible. We settled quickly on the new Bresson, *Au Hasard Balthazar*. You knew where you were – or at least where you were expected to be – with Bresson. Gritty, independent-minded, and shot in intellectual black-and-white; that's what they said about his films.

The cinema was near, gave a student reduction even on the evening show, and had enough right-looking people gazing at the stills outside. There was the usual array of hideous cartoon commercials, featuring animals of unidentifiable species. During my favourite commercial, the one with a squeaky matron urging *'Demandez Nuts'*, I was forced to suppress my normal, knowing, lubricious Anglo-Saxon giggle. I thought out a remark comparing English and French commercials, but was short of a word so didn't bother to launch it. That was another advantage of going to the cinema.

As we came out, I allowed the customary minute for us to get over our too-moved-to-speak reactions, then

'What did you think?' (Always get this in first)

'Very sad. And very true. Lots of ... '

'Integrity?'

'Yes, that's right, integrity. Honesty. But lots of humour, too. But a sad humour.'

You can't go wrong with integrity. It's a good thing to admire. Bresson had so much of it that once, when trying to film the silence of some mournful wood, he sent men out with guns to shoot the jarringly cheerful birds. I told Annick this story, and we agreed we didn't know quite what to make of it. Did he do it because he found it was impossible to simulate a birdless wood by running a blank tape? Or out of some deep, puritanical sense of honesty?

'Perhaps he just didn't like birds?' I quipped, having breathed the sentence over to myself beforehand, so that I could throw it off lightly.

At that stage, every laugh counts double, every smile is a reason for sweaty self-congratulation.

We flâned (we really did) our way to a bar, knocked off a couple of drinks, and I walked her to a bus stop. We'd chatted a fair amount and, during the permitted portions of silence, I'd been worrying about etiquette. We'd managed to cross the *vous/tu* barrier almost without noticing it, though as much in acknowledgment of student conventions as anything. But what, I wondered, about the first kiss? And anyway, would it, could it come so soon? I hadn't a clue about French customs, though I knew not to ask: *baiser*, after all, meant fuck as well as kiss in French. Quite what was expected or permitted, I had no idea. Toni and I once had a rhyme

> A kiss on the first,
> You can do your worst;
> A kiss on the second,
> No more than you reckoned!
> While a kiss on the third —
> You slow fucking turd!

– but this was written with the confidence of inexperience, and anyway, probably didn't apply outside the Home Counties. Then I realised – of course, use the local customs. Take advantage of the ubiquity of *le shake-hand*. Give her your paw, hold hers longer than necessary and then, with a slow, sensual, irresistible strength, draw her gradually towards you while gazing into her eyes as if you had just been given a copy of the first, suppressed edition of *Madame Bovary*. Good thinking.

Her bus drew up, I reached out an uncertain hand, she seized it quickly, dabbed her lips against my cheek before I saw what she was up to, released my slackened grasp, dug out her *carnet*, shouted '*A bientôt*', and was gone.

I'd kissed her! Hey, I'd kissed a French girl! She liked me! What's more, I hadn't even gone around for weeks beforehand finding out about her.

I watched as her bus drove off. If it had been one of the old-style buses, Annick could have been standing on the open platform, one hand clutching the rail, the other, palely lit by a solitary street lamp, raised in a fragile salute; she would have looked like some tearful emigrant at the stern of a departing ship. As it was, the pneumatic doors had shut her off from me with a clump of rubber, and she stayed invisible as the bus growled and throbbed off.

I walked to the Palais Royal feeling impressed with myself. I sat on a bench in the courtyard and inhaled the warm night. It felt as if everything was coming together, all at once. The past was all around; I was the present; art was here, and history, and now the promise of something much like love or sex. Over there in that corner was where Molière worked; across there, Cocteau, then Colette; there Blücher lost six million at roulette and for the rest of his life flew into a rage when the name of Paris was mentioned; there the first *café mécanique* was opened; and there, over there, at a little cutler's in the Galerie de Valois, Charlotte Corday bought the knife with which she killed Marat. And bringing it all together, ingesting it, making it mine, was me – fusing all the art and the history with what I might soon, with luck, be calling the life. The Gautier which Toni and I quoted to each other at school sidled into my head –

'*Tout passe*', it murmured. Maybe, I replied, but not for quite a bloody long time; not if I have anything to do with it.

I must write to Toni.

I did; but he hid any avuncular pleasure he might have felt.

> Dear Chris,
>
> *C'est magnifique, mais ce n'est pas la chair.* Get past the next set of lips and you might stir my interest. What have you been reading, what have you seen, and what, not who, have you been doing? You do realise, I hope, that Spring is not officially over yet, that you are in Paris, and that if I catch you anywhere near completing the cliché you can count on my lasting contempt. What about the strikes?
>
> Toni.

I suppose he was right; in any case, the sickly gushiness of my own letter can readily be inferred from the tone of his reply. But by the time it arrived it was out of date.

I lost my virginity on the 25th May 1968 (is it odd to remember the date? Most women remember theirs). You'll want to hear the details. Hell, *I* wouldn't mind hearing the details again; I don't come out of this part all that badly.

It was only our third night out together.

I think that deserves a paragraph to itself. At the time it was a matter of quaint pride to me, as if I'd actually planned it that way. I hadn't, of course.

The pre-bed stuff was almost completely non-verbal, though probably not for the same reason on each side. We'd been to the flicks again: an oldie this time, *Les Liaisons Dangereuses*, the Vadim modern-dress version with Jeanne Moreau and (to our joint delight), lurking sardonically in the shadows, Boris Vian.

When we came out I mentioned, in a formally casual way, the stock of calvados at my place. Its proximity was known.

The flat was as I'd left it, which means as I'd half-arranged it. Reasonably tidy, but not obsessive either way. Books lying open as if in use (some of them were – all the best lies have an alloy of truth). Lighting low and from the corners – for obvious reasons, but also in case some eager, treacherous spot had come into bud during the course of the film. Glasses put away, but rewashed first, and rinsed not dried, so that the calvados wouldn't have to be drained through its usual bobbing scum of tea-towel.

As we walked in, I casually tossed my jacket on to the armchair, so that when I invited Annick to sit down she would probably choose the sofa (she'd hardly go for the bed, despite its daytime disguise under an Indian coverlet and heap of cushions). If I was going to make a courting lunge at some stage, I didn't want to get smacked in the belly by the arm of the chair. These thoughts weren't really as brutal as they sound; they rented space in my mind in a provisional, hesitant way, and their tenancy made me feel slightly guilty. But I was thinking in the future conditional rather than the plain future; it's the tense which minimises responsibility.

So there we were, me in the chair, she on the sofa; sitting, sipping and looking. There was no gramophone in the flat; 'Shall we play the fruit machine?' seemed inappropriate. So we looked. I kept on not quite thinking of things to say. I wondered for a minute or two whether *l'amour libre* was the right translation for free love; and I'm glad I never found an answer.

Does one always think, on such occasions, that the other person is much more at ease than you are? In this case, as far as I was actively thinking about Annick, I assumed that, given her better command of the local language she would, if she had anything she wanted to say, speak. She didn't; I didn't; and what gradually emerged was something different in quality from a mere extended pause in the conversation. It was agreed silence, combined with total concentration on the other person; the result was more erotic than I knew was possible. The force of this silence came from its spontaneity. Subsequently, if ever I've tried to re-create the effect, it's always failed.

We were, perhaps, six feet apart, and fully dressed, but the subtlety and strength of our erotic interchange were greater than much I subsequently came to know in the hurried, fiercer world of naked hand-to-hand. It wasn't the sort of rough eye-gazing which passes for foreplay in the cinema. We started, admittedly, with each other's eyes and face, but soon strayed, if always returning. Each ocular foray into a new area produced a new scurry of excitement; each twitch of muscle, each flicker at the corner of the mouth, each shift of the fingers across the face had a particular, tender, and, as it seemed at the time, unambiguous significance.

We stayed like that for at least an hour, and afterwards we went to bed. It was a surprise. I won't say a disappointment, because it was too interesting for that; but it was a surprise. The bits I'd looked forward to were almost a let-down; the bits I hadn't known about were fun. In terms of penile pleasure there wasn't much that was new; and the dominant features of our brief tussle were curiosity and awkwardness. But the other bits ... the bits they never tell you about ... that mixture of power, tenderness and sheer cocky glee which comes with the total offer of a woman's body – why hadn't I read about that before? And why didn't they tell you about the football fan in the back of your skull, the man with the rattle and the scarf who shouts Yippee and stamps his feet on the terraces? And then, behind it all, there's that funny sense of having discharged a social burden; as if, at last, you've finally joined the human race; as if, after all, you won't now die a wholly ignorant man.

Afterwards (that was a word which meant so much as a kid, a word which, catching you unexpectedly out of a wash of prose, could bring you up short with a hard-on, a word which, above all others, I had wanted to be able to write about myself); afterwards, when the fan at the back of the skull had put down his rattle and tucked away his scarf and the terraces had gone quiet; afterwards, then, I slipped off to sleep murmuring to myself, 'Afterwards ... afterwards ... '

The letter I wrote to Toni the next morning has been lost (or so he says); perhaps he's being kind in not reminding me of the extravagant glee of my prose. I've still got his reply, though.

Dear Chris,
    I have ironed the bunting, put the flags to air, set a fuse

to the Thames, laid in the red paint. So you finally got them off. To borrow, or rather steal (since I'm sure she doesn't want it back), a phrase from a girl friend's letter which I was once posting for her and came unsealed in my hand, you have 'laid down the burden of your virginity'. What a hoot. You are now allowed to read *Les Fleurs du Mal* in the grown-up edition and I can tell you a pun I made up the other day – '*Elle m'a dit des maux d'amour*'. Is it still grammatical this way round? I can't remember any more.

That said, or rather *cela dit*, I must out of friendship (not to say a duty to the truth) tell you that while the content of your letter brought me relief, for which much thanks, the tone left something to be desired. I liked the observation bits, but, well, to put it bluntly, you don't have to fall in love, you know. It's not necessarily a package deal, you know, really. Just because you've gushed in one direction, it doesn't mean you have to in another as well. I expect you don't want to hear any of this, and I'm sure it's a waste of time – either you don't need to be told, or else you won't listen. But even if you won't listen to me, remember the old Froggy proverb (which I'll translate for your besotted mind), In love there is always one who kisses and one who offers the cheek. By the way, would you like me to send you any Durex?

Be bad, and have one for me,

Love,

Toni.

It was the sort of letter you half-read, smile at, and put aside. There's some point in advising the totally inexperienced; but advice to those on whom life has turned either sour or ridiculously sweet – it's a waste of postage. Besides, Toni and I were beginning to drift apart. The enemies who had given us common cause were no longer there; our adult enthusiasms were bound to be less congruent than our adolescent hates.

So, the only advice I was open to at the time was,

'No, not like that.'

'Sorry. Like this?'

'Almost ... '

'Well, it'll only be luck if I get it right you know.'

'More like this.'

'Oh, *I* see. You mean ... '

'Mmmm.'

And, in due course, I was mmmming and aaahing myself. Practical stuff, I began to discover, really was different from written stuff. At school, of course, we'd done all the necessary reading. We'd pored over *Lady C.* and dreamed of breasts hanging down above our heads like bells, and raindrops glistening during atavistic entwinings. We'd absorbed the great classics of Indian literature (and, as a result, practised PT a lot more energetically for some months, with a heaving sense of anticipation). We'd wondered, half-scared, about unguents.

I can't say that the texts we studied did us any harm; all I'd reproach them for is their misleading implications about the layout and functioning of muscles and tendons. The first time I tried anything remotely exploratory with Annick (I didn't particularly want to; just felt that if I didn't I might be thought someone with no sense of natural, inner rhythm), I got a shock. I'd been lying on top of her in what I would dismissively have called the missionary position (nowadays I reckon that the missionaries knew a thing or two) and decided to swing myself, casually and spontaneously, into the astride-kneeling-position. I swung my right leg out over Annick's left, bent it up, and smiled at her. Then I tried to move my left leg. I had just got it on top of her right one, when the movement sent me pitching forward, my head landing square on her ear as she tried to twist out of the way of my involuntary butt. My left groin was being torn open, my cock was trapped and near to snapping point, my right leg frozen at an untenable position, my eyes, nose and mouth were put out of action by the engulf-ing pillow, and my arms capable of pushing only in unhelpful directions.

'Sorry, did I hurt you,' I mumbled as I twisted my head sideways (ow, again) and got some air.

'You nearly broke my nose.'

'Sorry.'

'What were you trying to do?'

'I was trying to do this ... ooowwwww.'

I was stranded again, though this time my discouraged cock slipped out, and I keeled slowly over on my side.

'Oh, I see.'

She tucked me back in, twisted and raised her body slightly as I moved each leg in turn, and suddenly we were there. We were doing it! We were doing a position! Astride-kneeling – it worked! The man with the football rattle was delighted. Two, four, six, eight, who do we appreciate?

'Why did you want to do that?' Annick asked with a smile as I sat on top of her, grinning. (Oh God, maybe you shouldn't do it that way, not even with fully-lapsed Catholics.) But no; her smile was one of puzzled tolerance.

'I thought it might be nice,' I answered. Then, more honestly, 'I read about it.'

She smiled.

'And is it?' She pushed some hair off her face.

(Well, it wasn't painful, but on the other hand I suppose it wasn't actively nice. Your legs were in too great a state of tension; you felt like a posing muscle-man, each cubic inch strained for the judge's approval. On top of which, you couldn't, I suddenly realised, move an inch. All the work would have to be done by your partner.)

'I'm not sure.'

'Did it say in the book it was nice?'

'I don't remember. It just said it was one of the things you could do. They wouldn't have put it in if it wasn't nice, would they?'

I wondered privately whether this was one of those positions improved by the use of an unguent. Then, the solemnity in my voice became too much for Annick; she started laughing, I started laughing, my cock inevitably flopped out when attacked by such unfamiliar muscle spasms, and we rolled off into a hug.

This amused honesty, when I reflected on it later, was what started my mind off on serious thoughts: those thoughts which chase their own tails. On the nights I was sleeping alone I would interrogate myself, pry for signs and hints; I would lie awake with my questions about love, and then deduce love from my own wakefulness.

When I was with her, though, it was different, easy. Her honesty was infectious, too; though in my case I suspect it was as much a function of the nerves as of the intellect. Annick was the first person with whom I truly relaxed. Previously I had — even with Toni — been just honest for effect, competitively candid. Now, though the effect may have been the same to the outside observer, inside it felt different.

It was, I discovered, surprisingly easy to slip into this new mode; though it needed a push. On the third night we spent together, as we were undressing, Annick asked,

'What did you do on the first morning after I'd stayed here?' My confusion was momentarily covered by the process of taking my trousers off; but as I hesitated, she went on,

'And what did you feel?'

That was even harder. Couldn't very well admit to a mixture of gratitude and smugness, I thought.

'I wanted you to go so that I could write down what happened,' I offered cautiously.

'Can I read it?'

'Christ, no. Well, not yet anyway. Maybe some time.'

'OK. And what did you feel?'

'Smugness and gratitude. No, in the other order. You?'

'I felt amused, at sleeping with an Englishman, and relieved that you could speak French, and guilty about what my mother would say, and eager to tell my friends what had happened, and … interested.'

I then made some stumbling, embarrassed remarks in praise of her sincerity, and asked her how she had taught herself to act as she did.

'What do you mean, taught? It's not something you learn. Either you say what you mean or you don't. That's all.'

That sounded rather less than all at first; but gradually I understood. The key to Annick's candour was that there was no key. It was like the atom bomb: the secret is that there is no secret.

Until I met Annick I'd always been certain that the edgy cynicism and disbelief in which I dealt, plus a cowed trust in the word of any imaginative writer, were the only tools for the painful, wrenching extraction of truths from the surrounding quartz of hypocrisy and deceit. The pursuit of truth had always seemed something combative. Now, not exactly in a flash, but over a few weeks, I wondered if it weren't something both higher – above the supposed conflict – and simpler, attainable not through striving but a simple inward glance.

Annick taught me honesty (at least the principle of it); she helped me learn about sex; in return I taught her – well, certainly nothing that could be encompassed by an abstract noun. After a while, this became a joke between us, a confirmation of national character: the French deal in the abstract, the theoretical, the generality; the English in the detail, the gloss, the rider, the exception, the particularity. We didn't think it more than a half-truth on any wider scale, but in our own individual case it seemed to fit.

'What do you think of Rousseau?' I'd ask her; or existentialism; or the role of the cinema in society; or the theory of humour; or the process of decolonisation; or the mythification of De Gaulle; or the duty of the citizen in time of war; or the principles of neoclassical art; or Hegelian theory? She seemed at first dauntingly well-educated in the French manner, handling theories as easily as she forked spaghetti, backing her opinions with quotes, moving confidently from one discipline to another.

It was weeks before I finally got round the back of her defences in any substantial way; and by that time my belief in a British system of haphazard personal insight – the Constructive Loaf *en gros* – had been shaken. We were discussing Rimbaud, when suddenly I began to notice that all the quotes she used to support her argument for Rimbaud as the self-destructive Romantic (as opposed to my version of him as the second modern poet after Baudelaire) came from the same poems: *Le Bateau Ivre*, *Voyelles* and *Ophélie*. Had she read *Les Illuminations*?

'No.'

Had she read the *Letters*?

'No.'

Had she read the rest of his poems?

'No.'

Better and better; I pressed the advantage home. She hadn't read *Ce qu'on dit au poète à propos des fleurs*; she hadn't read *Les Déserts de l'Amour*; she hadn't even read *Une Saison en Enfer*. She certainly didn't understand '*JE est un autre*'. When I'd finished, Annick asked,

'Feeling better?'

'What a relief. I thought you knew everything.'

'No. It's just that I say what I know, and no more, no less.'

'Whereas I … ?'

'You know things you don't say.'

'And say things I don't know?'

'Of course; that goes without saying.'

Second lesson. After honesty of response, honesty of expression. But how had the conversation been turned? I thought I was coming out on top and suddenly here I was back on the mat again, a manicured thumb prising out my jelly eyeball.

'Why do you always come out on top?'

'I don't. I just learn silently. You learn melodramatically, by instruction not observation. And you like to be told you're learning.'

'Why are you so unbearably assured?'

'Because you think I am.'

'Why do I think you are?'

'Because I never ask questions. "In life, there are only two real characters, the questioner and the answerer".'

'Who said that?'

'He asked. Guess.'

'No.'

'All right. Oscar Wilde – in translation, of course? Victor Hugo? D'Alembert?'

'I don't really want to know.'

'Yes you do. Everyone always does.'

'Anyway, I think it's a crappy quote. I bet you made it up yourself.'

'Of course I did.'

'I thought so.'

We stared at each other, excited a little by our first wrangle. Annick pushed her hair back off her right cheek, opened her mouth, and, in a parody of cinematic sensuality, ran the tip of her tongue across her top lip. She said gently,

'Vauvenargues.'

'Vauvenargues! Christ, I've never read him. I've only just heard of him.' Annick licked her bottom lip as well.

'You bitch! I bet that's the only line of Vauvenargues you know. I bet you got it out of Bédier-Hazard.'

' "*Il faut tout attendre et tout craindre du temps et des hommes*".'

'*Et des femmes.*'

' "*Il vaut mieux ...* " '

'OK, OK, I surrender. I don't want to hear any more. You're a genius, you're the Bib Nat!'

Defeat once used to make me cry; now it made me grumpy and aggressive. I looked at her and thought, I could easily dislike you.

Her hair had fallen down over her face again. She pushed it away, and parted her lips once more. It may still have been parody, but if it was, you could still take it straight. I took it straight.

When we had finished making love, she rolled away from me, over on to her left side. I squinted across at her small frame and gently heaving back, and felt weeks older. How strange that Time did these sudden rabbit-hops; at this rate I'd soon have matured all the way up to my real age. I watched a patch of freckles rise and fall and remembered the quaint, despairing fantasies Toni and I had elaborated. Now, the likelihood of castration by Nazi X-ray seemed really very remote, the theory of SST arid and academic. Pre-marital sex – a triple-épat, a double-écras at school – suddenly didn't feel as if it had anything to do with the bourgeoisie. And what about the structuring of the decades? If it were true, I'd only have one more year of Sex before plunging into thirty years of alternating War and Austerity. There didn't seem much probability of that.

Beside me, Annick was dreaming; a sigh of puzzled pain escaped from her. This is what it's all about, I thought: an argument over Rimbaud (which I'd won – well, more or less), sex *in the afternoon*, a girl asleep, and me here – awake, on watch, observing. I crept out of bed, found my sketch pad, and made a painstaking drawing of Annick. Then I signed and dated it.

3 · Redon, Oxford

I went to Paris determined to immerse myself in the culture, the language, the street-life, and – I would doubtless have added, with hesitant casualness – the women. At first, I deliberately avoided English people, papers and books; my tongue refused anglicisms as it did whisky or Coca-Cola. I began to gesture: just as the tongue and lips are given more work by the precise placing of French vowels, so the hands are expected to go new places too. I brushed the side of my jaw with the backs of my fingers to indicate boredom. I learned to shrug up my shoulders while turning down my mouth. I linked my fingers in front of my stomach, palms turned inwards, then sprang both thumbs out while making a plopping noise with my lips. This last gesture – meaning roughly 'Search me' – would have been ridiculed at school. I did it rather well.

Yet the better I got at talking, gesturing and immersion, the more inner resistance built up to the whole process. Years later, I read about a Californian experiment on Japanese-born GI brides. There was a large colony of such women, who still spoke Japanese as regularly as English: Japanese in the shops and amongst themselves, English at home. The women were interviewed about their lives twice, the first time in Japanese, the second in English. The results showed that in Japanese, the women were submissive, supportive creatures, aware of the value of tight social cohesion; in English, they were independent, frank, and much more outward-looking.

I'm not saying anything quite as bisecting as this happened to me. But after a while I definitely became aware, if not of saying things I didn't believe, at least of saying things I didn't know I'd thought in ways I hadn't previously considered. I found myself more prone to generalisation, to labelling and ticketing and docketing and sectioning and explaining and to lucidity – God, yes, to lucidity. I felt a kind of internal stirring; it wasn't loneliness (I had Annick), it wasn't homesickness, it was something to do with being English. I felt, too, as if one part of me was being faintly disloyal to another part.

One afternoon, when querulously conscious of this resented metamorphosis, I went to visit the Musée Gustave Moreau. It's an unwelcoming place near the Gare Saint-Lazare which closes for an extra rogue day in the middle of the week (as well as for the whole of August) and so has even fewer visitors than you might expect; you tend to hear about it on your third visit and get around to going on your fourth. Stacked to the ceiling with pictures and drawings, it was left to the State by Moreau when he died, and has been grudgingly kept up ever since. It was one of my favourite haunts.

I offered the blue-uniformed *gardien* my student card, as I'd already done several times that spring. He never recognised me, and went through the same ritual every time. He would be sitting at his desk, a cigarette in his right hand held below the level of the top, and a *Série Noire* pressed down in front of him by his left hand. Such is the hierarchy of bureaucratic offences. He'd look up, see a customer, pull open his top drawer with the last two fingers of his right hand, deposit the loose, wet, oval fag on an ash-tray, close the drawer, turn over the *Série Noire* on to its stomach, press it down even flatter, reach for his roll of tickets, murmur 'No reduction', tear off a ticket, push it in front of me, take my three francs, shove across fifty centimes change, pick my ticket up again, tear it in half, drop one part of it in his waste-paper basket and return the other to me. By the time I had a foot on the stairs the smoke would be rising again and the book turned over.

Upstairs was a huge, high barn of a studio, inadequately

heated by a chunky black central stove which must have been inadequately heating it ever since Moreau's time. Around the walls hung finished and half-finished paintings, many of them enormous and all complex, involving that odd mixture of private and public symbolism which at the time I found so beguiling. Large wooden chests with thin drawers, like massive butterfly cabinets, contained scores of preliminary drawings. You pulled out the drawers and squinted through your own reflection in the covering glass at faint pencilled swoops and dips, studded here and there with details that would later be transformed into golds and silvers, flashing head-dresses, breastplates, bejewelled girdles, encrusted swords, and all worked into a new and burnished version of the antique or the scriptural: laced with eroticism, tinged with necessary violence, coloured with a palette of controlled excess.

'Wanker's art, isn't it?' An English voice, blatantly unhushed, shot across the bare boards from the other side of the studio. I went back to studying a pen-and-ink drawing for 'The Suitors'; then another, in sepia, heightened with white.

'It's weird. It's really surreal. What a taste in women. Amazons.' This was a different voice, again a man's, but slower, deeper, more ready to admire. I looked into a few more butterfly cabinets, but my attention wasn't wholly on the drawings. I could hear the philistines – their pockets still bulging with duty-free – creaking their way slowly round the other side of the studio.

'But it's whack-off art, isn't it?' (first voice again) 'It's all just wrist stuff.'

'Well, dunno,' (second voice) 'I mean, he's got lots to say, hasn't he? That arm there's rather good.'

'None of your aesthetic rubbish here, Dave.'

'It is a bit self-indulgent,' (third voice, a girl's, quiet but high in pitch) 'but we're coming to it a bit cold, aren't we? There's a lot of context we ought to know about, I expect. Do you think that's Salomé?'

'Dunno.' (second voice) 'Why's she got his head on a zither? I thought she carried it round on a tray.'

'Poetic licence?' (girl)

'Could be.' (second voice – 'Dave' – again) 'Doesn't look like Egypt in the background, though, does it? And who are those poofy shepherds?'

That was enough. I turned round and gave them a blast – in French of course. With all the abstract nouns it sounded quite heightened and professional. Wanking, as far as I knew, was *la masturbation*, and there's a lot of vowel richness in the word, which always helps when you're trying to inject contempt. I took them apart over Salomé, who was of course a Thracian woman with the head of Orpheus. I threw in Mallarmé, and Chassériau, to whom Moreau was apprenticed, and Redon, whose vapid, washy maunderings are called symbolist by some, but who is as far from Moreau as Burne-Jones is from Holman Hunt.

There was a pause. The three of them, no older than me, stood there looking puzzled. The first voice, a sort of tough-looking runt in a brown leather jacket and frayed jeans, turned to the second, taller but weaker-looking, with conventional English clothes (tweed jacket, V-neck pullover, tie), and said,

'Get any of that, Dave?'

'All Greek to me.' Then, belying his apparent mildness, he looked at me, said loudly, 'Verdun', and drew his forefinger across his throat.

'Get any of it, Marion?' She was about the same height as leatherjacket, with one of those pinkish, freckled and faintly furry English complexions; her manner, though quiet, seemed direct.

'Some of it,' she said. 'But I think it was all an act anyway.'

'Whaffor?'

'I think he's probably English.'

I pretended not to understand. Leatherjacket and Dave prowled round me like pygmies with a television explorer. I felt my clothes being looked over, then my hair, then the book in my hand. It was Jean Giono's *Colline*, so I felt OK; when they saw that I had seen them looking, I held it up to them. Leatherjacket studied it.

'Pardong, Mossoo, but are you actuellement a Brit?'

I waved the book at him again, for fear I might laugh. I was nervily puritanical about clothes at that time. Any departure from a neat conventional style of dressing indicated, as far as I was concerned, parallel departures from reason, lucidity, trustworthiness and emotional stability. I rarely stayed around long enough to question my prejudices; still, here was a man in fraying, faded jeans nearly making me laugh. What an odd trio: this fellow, a girl who didn't have any make-up on at all as far as I could see, and 'Dave', who looked, well, almost as if he could have been a friend of mine.

'Je suis practically sure que c'est un Brit.' Dave this time. Leatherjacket fingered my lapel.

'Pouvez-vous ... ' and Dave seized him suddenly, and swung him off into a clumping, camping waltz. The girl looked at me in an entirely pleasant fashion. No, she didn't have any make-up; but on the other hand, she looked OK without it. How curious.

'What are you doing over here?' she asked.

'Oh, this and that. Bit of research, bit of writing, bit of having a change from having to do things. And you?'

'Holiday for a few weeks.'

'And them?'

'Dave works over here in a bank. Mickey's doing research at the Courtauld; that's why we're here.'

'Oh really?' (Oh Christ) 'What into?'

'Moreau, actually.' She smiled.

'Oh Christ. And I suppose his French is pretty good ... '

'His mother was French.'

Oh well, you lose some, you lose some, as we would have said at school. Dave and Mickey came clockworking back, humming the Blue Danube.

'Well, Marion?'

'He is French after all,' she replied, smiling again, 'but his English is jolly good.'

'Eep eep ourah,' shouted Dave, 'Tott-en'am 'Ot-spure. Mi-chel Ja-zy. Bobb-ee Moiré. I kees you both sheek.'

He didn't, fortunately. The *gardien* had got to the top of the stairs, *Série Noire* still in his left hand. He threw us out.

We went to a bar and had a drink. Gradually we ironed out who was French and who English, despite Dave's curious method of conversation, which consisted largely of proper names pronounced in a heavy French (or Franche, as he would say) accent, accompanied by a semi-hysterical gesture. Marion offered no behavioural mannerisms one could grab hold of – whatever was said, she remained quiet, direct, open, bright. Mickey was the hardest to master, though. Ego, charm, competitiveness, and a certain cunning, which made him pretend to know less than he did until he'd found out roughly how much you knew. The sort of character who makes me react by being academic, diffident, wry if possible, but basically straight.

'You're, um, working on Moreau, I gather?' was my first halting, peace-making move.

'More like he's working on me. Cross-buttock and body-slam, and when you've got that weight on top of you, you submit.'

Dave looked ready to come up with an impression, but couldn't think of which bit of a wrestler to do.

'But why don't you like him?'

'It's all academic wanking, isn't it, as I seem to have said before? I mean, the idea of academic symbolism, it's fucking ridiculous, isn't it?'

'It's an oxymoron.'

'I'll buy the last part. But he's so earthbound. He's clever, and can paint, and odd, I'll give you that. But he's frozen – it's like his colours, they look as if they're bright and weird, but in fact they're actually rather dull if you look at them.'

'Not like ... '

'Not like Redon. Quite.'

'Redon,' went Dave, 'Redon. Oxfor', Bah-nbri, Bur-meeng'am. *Changez, changez.*' He whistled and chuffed.

'Why are you working on him then?'

'It's the grant, man, the grant. It's got me right here ...

aaaaargh.' He gurgled as he clutched at his heart, acting fatally wounded. Dave leaned over him, pressed his ear to his chest.

'You gotta tell me, Doc,' Mickey panted in a wrecked way, 'you gotta tell me. Am I hurt bad?'

Dave pulled up one of Mickey's eyelids, slapped him round the face a few times, and listened again. Marion watched impassively. Dave put on a frown.

'Well, you're an intelligent man; I think you can face the truth. It's serious, certainly, but probably not fatal. You have a displaced bill-fold and your credit has crumpled in under the pressure. You have this draining problem, but I think I'll be able to put in a plug.'

'Thanks, Doc, you're a pal. I couldn't have taken it from anyone else.' They stopped and looked at me. I said nothing, wondering what was going on.

'You realise, of course,' Dave went on, 'that you're suffering from acute alcohol shortage?'

'Oh no, Doc, do you mean I could ...'

'Afraid so. It's one of the acutest cases I've seen for some time. Just take a look at this.' He held up Mickey's empty glass.

'No, no, no, I won't, I can't,' Mickey began to shout, hiding his head in his arms.

'You must look,' Dave said firmly. 'You must face these things.' Gradually, he began to prise Mickey's arms away from his head. He held up the glass in front of the patient's eyes. Mickey did a faint.

I got the point. I would have done so earlier if I hadn't been watching the play. It was my round.

4 · Beatific Couples

When I wasn't with Annick, or wandering the streets looking to catch life on the hip – that sudden nun, the *clochard* with *Le Monde*, the monstrous sadness of a barrel organ – I was with Mickey, Dave and Marion. In a month together they had become inseparable. I made the natural comparison with *Jules et Jim*; Mickey replied, with an unsettling candour, that he had landed the Jeanne Moreau part. It was true: he was the instigator, the provoker, the one for whose attention the other two competed. Dave competed by joining in, Marion by pretending to stand apart. Uncertain of my status, I tagged along with them on rounds of cafés, return visits to the Musée Gustave Moreau (the *gardien* never recognised us), and sudden trips out of Paris to the edge of the Beauce, or to the mad, polychrome chocolate factory at Noisiel.

Marion was believed by her parents to be taking a course which the organisers – with Gallic modesty – called *Civilisation*: chunks of Descartes, lectures on the Code Napoléon, sessions of Rameau, coach-tours of Versailles and Sèvres. Marion frequently tempted herself with reasons for staying away. Lunch with me was one more easy reason.

We began meeting every few days at a little café-restaurant called Le Petit Coq near the République (Métro: Filles du Calvaire); we lunched off long, tubular sandwiches the size of small dachshunds. It wasn't an amorous conspiracy; we met because we had time on our hands. We discussed Mickey and Dave a lot. I would practise my new-found candour and offer frowningly serious analyses of my shifting responses to them;

Marion was more reticent in judgment, but also more generous. She was, I noted, practical in her thoughts, sharp on both vagueness and pretension. She was easy to talk to; but also had an unsettling habit of asking me questions which I imagined I had escaped from, and wouldn't have to put up with again before my return to England.

'What are you going to do, then?' she once asked, over our third or fourth lunch.

(Do? What was I going to do? What could she mean? Was she asking for a pass? Surely not here; though she was looking pretty today, her boyishly cropped hair newly washed, and a pinky-brown dress tightly gathered at all the nice places. Do? She couldn't actually mean ...)

'You mean ... with ... my life?' I half-giggled, waiting for her to join in.

'Of course. What's funny?'

'Well, it's funny that you're the first person of my own age who's actually ever asked that. It's so ... authoritarian.'

'Sorry, I'm not meaning to sound authoritarian; just curious. I wondered if you'd ever asked yourself the question.'

I'd never needed to, that was part of the trouble – I was always getting asked it by others. When I was a child, the question always came down at me vertically, from above, along with orange ten-shilling notes at Christmas and Boots tokens and strange powders and scents and the occasional swipe. When I was an adolescent, it came from a different (but still downward) angle, from concerned masters armed with pamphlets and the word 'life', which they pronounced as if it were an item of Corps uniform. Finally, when I was a student, the question came horizontally, from parents sharing a bottle of wine, from tutors sharing a manly sex joke, once from a girl who thought that it would act as an anaphrodisiac. When, I wondered, would the angle change; when would I find myself looking down on the question?

'Well, I suppose my problem's always been the short term. There are quite a lot of jobs I wouldn't mind ending up with. I wouldn't mind running the BBC, for instance, and I'd like to have my own publishing firm and an art gallery on the side while of course always leaving time to lead the RPO. Then I wouldn't mind being a General in a sort of way, and there's the Cabinet, though I think I'll keep that up my sleeve in case all else fails. I'd *quite* like to run a cross-Channel ferry, and architecture is definitely a possibility, and you think I'm joking but you'd be surprised that I'm not really.'

Marion just looked at me, half smiling, half impatient.

'I mean I am up to a point, but then again I'm not. One problem is, I sometimes don't feel I'm quite the right age. Do you have that?'

'No.'

'I mean, you may happen to think I'm rather immature, but actually I often don't feel quite at ease with the age I've got. Sometimes, in a funny sort of way, I long to be a sprightly sixty-five. You don't have that?'

'No.'

'It's as if everyone has a perfect age to which they aspire, and they're only truly at ease with themselves when they get there. I suppose with most people it's between twenty-five and thirty-five, so the question doesn't really arise, or if it does it's in a disguised form: when they've passed thirty-five they assume their disgruntlement comes from being middle-aged and seeing senility and death on the way. But it also comes from leaving behind their perfect age.'

'How very odd. Fancy looking forward to bed bottles and tripping over paving stones.'

'I said a sprightly sixty-five.'

'Oh, so it's going to be all country walks and reading Peacock by the fire and having adoring grandchildren making you muffins?'

'I don't know. I don't have a specific fantasy image. I just have a feeling. But only sometimes.'

'Maybe you can't face the struggle to make a living.'

'Why do you think there is a struggle?' (Hah, not letting her get away with that one too easily. Just because she wants to be a civil servant or something.)

'Well, how are you going to support your wife and children?'

'Where, where?' I did the panicky, over-the-shoulder look. I could see nothing more realistic than two kids in Start-Rite shoes, satchels on their shoulders, gazing at the long road ahead. Certainly no wife, no picture of a wife. What did Marion think she was up to? She could lay off, you know, if she wanted to. 'Give me time, give me time.'

'Why?' (The funny thing was, her manner wasn't hectoring at all; it was quite amiable – but just fucking persistent.)

'I'm only twenty-one. I mean, I'm still … '

'Still what?'

'Well, still having relationships.'

'In the plural?'

'Well, not simultaneously, of course not.'

'Why not?' (Why could I never predict the way the conversation was going?)

'Well, I suppose I may have discarded Christian sexual ethics, but I do believe in being faithful to one person at a time.'

'That's a funny statement. Anyway, isn't marriage a relationship?'

'Of course. So what?'

'Well, you said that you were going to have relationships and then you were going to get married.'

'I didn't say I *was* going to get married.'

'Technically I suppose you didn't, no.' (Actually, I bloody didn't, either)

'But?'

She had put her head on one side and was pushing the crumbs of her lunch around the plate. Then she looked up. Why can you always tell when people are going to say nasty things to you?

'But you're not odd enough not to.'

'Anyway, it depends on … '

'The right girl at the right time at the right price?'

'Yes, I suppose so.'

'Don't you believe it. I daresay it happens sometimes, and I daresay that's what it looks like, or what you make it look like in retrospect. It's usually other things, though, isn't it?'

' ... ?'

'Opportunity, meal ticket, desire for children ... '

'Yes, I suppose so.'

' ... fear of ageing, possessiveness. I don't know, I think it often comes from a reluctance to admit that you've never in your life loved hard enough to end up married. A sort of misplaced idealism, really, a determination to prove that you're capable of the ultimate experience.'

'You know, you're much more sceptical than I thought I was.'

It was extraordinary. To hear a girl saying things like this, coming out with men's tough talk, the sort of remarks in which you only half believed yourself, but which were called for on various occasions. (Annick never spoke like this, and I thought she was uniquely honest.) But Marion talked without any bravado; she behaved as if she were making simple, incontestable observations. She was smiling at me again.

'I don't think I'm being cynical, if that's what you mean by saying sceptical.'

'But you've been reading La Rochefoucauld. *"Il y a certains gens ... " '*

'I know it. No, I haven't; I've been observing.' (She looked at me closely; she was nice to be looked at by) 'Before I came out here, a friend of mine got married. She was my age, he was about thirty. A week before the wedding, we were meant to be going to the cinema, the three of us, but she had a cold or something, so I went with him. We ended up talking about marriage. He said how he was looking forward to it and how he supposed it would be all right in the end, and you were bound to have your ups and downs – the usual stuff they all come out with; and then he said, "To be honest, it's obviously not the greatest love in the world".'

'How did you react?'

'I was shocked at first, partly because he was marrying my friend, but mainly because I found it hard to believe anyone could go into marriage without first persuading himself that no one had ever before loved as strongly as he was doing.'

'Did you tell your friend?'

'No. Because after I'd thought about it, I realised I wasn't shocked at all, that his remark was rather admirable. And that my friend probably had some similar reservation, but wasn't letting on. Anyway, they were both reasonable people and neither was feeble-minded or weak-willed, so I thought I didn't have the right to interfere.'

'Quite.'

'But it struck me later that, as they looked like any other beatific couple on their wedding day, other beatific couples probably had similar reservations.'

'The logic isn't faultless, you know.'

'No, but the observation is.'

'Yes, I suppose it may be.'

I didn't really have any grounds for dissent; I didn't even have any evidence of my own to offer.

There was a silence, as if there had been implications in the conversation which we hadn't admitted at the time, but which were now percolating through. I looked at her, and noticed the colour of her eyes for the first time: they were dark slate-grey, the colour of French roofs after rain. She wasn't smiling.

'Don't start reading things into this conversation,' she suddenly said.

'What do you mean?'

'Well, if you're starting to feel threatened, you might just decide I fancy you.'

' … '

'What's she like, just out of interest, the girl you're having a relationship with, as you put it?'

'What's odd about putting it that way? Annick.'

'Annick.'

What could I say? I felt that any description I gave would be a sort of betrayal; yet not to say anything would make it seem as if I were ashamed of her; even hesitating made it look as if I was doing a quiet mental cover-up.

'You don't have to tell me – it's none of my business after all.'

'No, no, I want to – or at any rate, I don't mind telling you. She's ... very direct, and ... um, emotional, and ... ' (Christ, what else?) ' ... and I don't lie to her.'

'It's OK.' Marion had got up, and was reaching into her purse for her share of the lunch bill. 'Don't bother, I won't embarrass you.'

I had, I realised, been blushing energetically. When asked to describe Annick, I could somehow only see her in the privacy of orgasm, with me plugged into her. Also I suddenly found it hard translating my time with her into unfamiliar English.

'I'm not embarrassed, I just ... '

She dropped a few francs on the table and left. I attacked my remaining slab of bread – a large, damp, unsalted, open-pored slice. Then I tried to skim off the last quarter-inch of coffee, but tangled with the grounds. Why was I so upset? Did I fancy Marion? Why had I felt I didn't want her to leave? That'd be something – fancying two people at once. And what about them fancying you? Though did she fancy me? Nice tits, I murmured nudgingly to myself; though, to tell the truth, I didn't really know whether they were nice or nasty. Yes I did, of course I did. They were nice because they existed. They were nice because they lived in a bra with hooks at the back and secret bits of elastic and straps you could occasionally glimpse. They were nice because they would probably turn out, if you were good, to have nipples at the end.

But I was only swaggering. What I'd noticed most about Marion was how direct, how uncomplicated she was. She seemed to exude psychic health; she made me feel slightly dishonest even when I was telling the truth. But then, Annick did the same. Was this a coincidence, or was it how all girls made you feel? And how to find out?

I paid the bill and flâned (though it's rather hard to do it by yourself) towards the Place de la République. Dumas *père* built his *théâtre historique* here, and put on his own plays. The public queued for two days to get into his first opening night; he had huge successes, yet in ten years the project made him bankrupt. There didn't seem to be times like that any more; times, or ambitions. Dumas would ride his horse into a stable, seize an overhead beam, grasp the horse tightly with his legs, and lift it off the ground. He also claimed to have 365 illegitimate children scattered round the world: one for every day of the year. The energy made you wince. But then, I reflected, as I headed down the Métro, the scale of the world has changed since those days. For a start, you didn't get marks for bastards any more.

5 · *Je t'aime bien*

Being asked to describe my relationship with Annick made me uneasy for another reason: I hadn't told her about Marion. She'd heard about my *trois amis anglais* – a usefully genderless expression – but not about my *tête-à-tête* lunches. Was there anything *to* tell? On the other hand, if there was nothing to tell, why did I feel shifty? Was it love, or guilt, or mere sexual gratitude? And why didn't I know: 'feelings' were things you felt, so why couldn't you identify them?

It was hard to know how to tell Annick about Marion. A simple statement of fact would look ridiculous; the truth would look like a lie. It would have to be slipped in casually after all. I practised saying *mon amie anglaise* to myself, and *une amie anglaise*, and *cette amie anglaise*. Mentioning the nationality would take the sting out of it.

A good opportunity seemed to arise over breakfast one morning (bowls of coffee and yesterday's bread heated up in the oven). We were discussing what to do that evening, and Annick had mentioned the new film by Melville.

'Oh, yes,' I said casually, '*mon amie anglaise* has seen it. She' (cunning confirmation of gender) 'thought it was quite good.' (Marion hadn't actually seen the film. Shit – a lie to tell the truth; where did this leave you?)

'OK, shall we go then?'

I thought I'd better make things quite clear.

'Yes, *mon amie anglaise* really thought it was quite good.'

'Fine, that's settled, then.'

It didn't seem to be settled to me. We didn't seem to be getting anywhere.

'*Mon amie anglaise* ... '

'You want to tell me something?'

' ... ?'

'Is this *le tact anglais*?' Annick lit her second cigarette of the breakfast. Christ, her mouth was turning down. She took two quick puffs. I hadn't seen this – almost fierceness – on her face before. This was new.

'What? No. What do you mean?'

'Do you want to tell me something?'

'Um ... this ... this film is ... apparently very good.'

'Yes. How do you know?'

'Oh, one of my friends told me.'

Genderless again; also hopeless. Instead of being casual and throwaway, it was coming out furtive and nervous.

'I thought you mentioned an English girl friend.'

'Uh, nnn, yes, I did. Why, don't you have any French boy friends?' (Altogether too hostile.)

'Yes, but I don't usually refer to one of them three times running unless I want to say something particular about him.'

'Well, I suppose all I wanted to say about ... about *cette amie anglaise* is that ... she's a friend.'

'You mean you're sleeping with her.' Annick stubbed out her cigarette and glared at me.

'NO. Of course not. I sleep with you.'

'So you do. I had noticed it from time to time. But not twenty-four hours a day.'

'I'm not ... perfidious.' (I couldn't think of the word for 'unfaithful'; for some reason, only *adultère* came into my head, which had quite the wrong implications.)

'Albion is always perfidious. We learn that at school.'

'And our books tell us the French are often jealous without reason.'

'But you might be giving me reason.'

'Of course not. *Je* ... '

'Yes?'

I was going to say *je t'aime*, but I couldn't bring myself to. After all, I hadn't really thought about it enough; and I wasn't going to be argued into saying what I thought should be offered calmly and soberly. Instead, I weakened it,

'*Je t'aime bien, tu sais.*'

'Of course you do! Of course. How rational, how measured, how English. You say it as if you'd known me for twenty years, not a few weeks. Why this deadly accuracy of emotion? Why this way of telling me you've had enough? Why not just write me a letter, that would be best of all. Write me a letter, as formal as you can make it, and have it signed by your secretary.'

She paused. I didn't know what to say. I was being accused of being honest: how ironic. I'd never known a girl rage at me like this before. Unexpected emotions left me puzzled. But at the same time the outburst gave me sudden jabs of pride: the pride of participation, and the pride of instigation. No matter that Annick's anger and distress were caused by my own incompetent misinformation: they're *mine* now. They're part of *me*, of *my* experience.

'I'm sorry.'

'You're not sincere.'

'I don't mean I'm sorry because I'm at fault, I mean I'm sorry that you've misunderstood the situation. I'm sorry that just because you've tried to teach me to say precisely what I feel and mean, I'm unable to satisfy your need for extravagant emotional gestures which have no veritable substance in real feelings.' It wasn't wholly honest, I suppose, but near enough to make no difference.

'I thought I was teaching you to be sincere, not to be cruel.'

That's a very French line, I thought (reverting under attack to Englishness and detachment). Then, suddenly, I noticed – my God, another first – she was crying.

'Don't cry,' I said, and the softness with which it came out quite took me by surprise. She went on crying. I couldn't help looking at her face and thinking, despite myself, what a lot less attractive it looked now; her mouth unkissable, her hair stuck together in places on her cheek by tears, and the contortions suddenly giving her pouches under her eyes and crow's-feet by her eyes. I couldn't think what to do. I got up, went round to her side of the table (pushing the butter out of range of her raking hair as I moved), and half-knelt, rather awkwardly, beside her. I couldn't stand and put my arm round her – that would seem patronising; I couldn't kneel completely – that would seem grovelling; so I ended up half-squatting with my arm just high enough to go round her shoulder.

'Why are you crying?' I asked, rather ineptly.

Annick didn't answer. Her shoulders kept heaving while she cried: was she just sobbing violently, or was she trying to throw my arm off her back? How could you tell? It was time to be sensitive, I thought. I did this by keeping a baffled silence for a bit. However, this became rather boring.

'Are you crying because I mentioned that girl?'

No reply.

'Are you crying because you don't think I love you enough?'

No reply. I was stumped.

'Are you crying because you love me?'

It was always a possibility, I thought.

Annick walked out at that point. She slid from under my arm, got up, picked her bag off the table, ignored her copy of *L'Express*, and was away before I could get up from my awkward position. Why couldn't I see her face as she left? I wondered. Why did she keep it down so that her hair fell over it? Had she finished with *L'Express*? Why had she left? And had she left, or had she really just gone off to work? How did I find that out? I could hardly ring her office and ask her to identify the category of her departure. I went to the fruit machine and fed in an old franc or two. You lose some, you lose some. I thought I felt like Humphrey Bogart.

So, for a change, I did some work myself; not in the Bib Nat, where there was an outside chance of running into Annick, but at the Musée du Théâtre. After a couple of hours shuffling through huge folders of largely unnamed actresses of the 1820s, I felt morally better and more sexually stable; maybe prints of long-dead women were what I got on with most easily.

After a quick *croque*, the sight of other, real people began to get me down again. I dropped in at the Rex-Alhambra where a Gary Cooper festival was showing. A couple of hours later, revived by the unreal, I felt able to go back to the flat. After all, she might be back there, ready to tell me how much she'd misunderstood me; then we could go to bed (the books said it was even better after a quarrel). On the other hand, she might be lying in wait with a gun or a knife (French cutlery seemed invented for the *crime passionnel*). There might be a note. Who knows, even a present?

There wasn't anything, of course. The flat was exactly as I'd left it. I kept looking for signs that Annick had secretly come back in the course of the day and moved something, tidied something, left a reminder of herself. But she hadn't. A half-smoked cigarette still lay on her breakfast plate, bent and wrinkled like a knuckle. There must be something she would have to come back for; but there wasn't – her overnight things had never been more than what would fit in her handbag. Still, she had taken her key, so it might mean she was coming back.

That evening I went to see the Melville we'd almost agreed to go and see. I hung around in the foyer until I'd missed the first ten minutes, then went in impatiently. But the impatience failed to cancel out the disappointment; I didn't enjoy the film.

The next morning in the post I got my key back, sellotaped to a piece of cardboard. I stuck my hand into every corner of the envelope, but there was nothing else.

I sat there for some time wondering about Annick. How much I loved her; whether I loved her. When I was a child, my white-haired, full-bosomed, duck-tending grandmother used to hold her arms out to us kids and say, 'How much do you love Granny?' The three of us, on cue, would stretch our arms out as far as they would go, cock our fingertips in slightly, and answer, 'This much.'

But measurement on a subtler scale than this – is it possible? Isn't it still a matter of some grand gesture, some apocalyptic assurance? And in any case, don't you need some scale of comparison to make measurements; how can you possibly judge on a first outing? I could have told Annick that I loved her more than my mother, just as I could have said that of all my girl friends she was the best in bed; but such praise would be valueless.

Well, what about the simple question, again, do I love her?

Depends what you mean by love. When do you cross the dividing line? When does *je t'aime bien* become *je t'aime*? The easy answer is, you know when you're in love, because there's no way you can doubt it, any more than you can doubt when your house is on fire. That's the trouble, though: try to describe the phenomenon and you get either a tautology or a metaphor. Does anyone feel any more that they are walking on air? Or do they merely feel as they think they would feel if they were walking on air? Or do they merely think they ought to feel as if they are walking on air?

Hesitancy doesn't indicate lack of feeling, just uncertainty about terminology (and, perhaps, the after-effects of my conversation with Marion). Doesn't the terminology affect the emotion in any case? Shouldn't I just have said *je t'aime* (and who's to say I wouldn't have been telling the truth)? Naming can lead to making.

These were my thoughts as I sat with the key in my hand.

I found that even thinking about semantics made me horny.

So maybe I did love her?

I certainly never saw her again.

After Annick left I found ways of not seeing *mes amis anglais*. I rediscovered, or at least pretended, a fair amount of interest in my research. I clocked in daily at the Bib Nat and worked my way through stacks of material, transcribing it dutifully on to index cards. It was the sort of subject which responded to honest slog plus an instinct for guessing where to look; mastery of the library's catalogue was at least half the key. There was little need for original thought, only for an ability to synthesise the observations of others. This had, of course, been part of the original plan: get something you can work at without using up the valuable parts of your head, and make sure you have lots of spare time.

In fact, my life became again what it had been when I first arrived in Paris. I went back to practising my memory exercises, which I had lately begun to ignore. Using them, I wrote a series of prose poems which I called *Spleenters*: urban allegories, sardonic character-sketches, elusive verse, and passages of straight descriptions, which gradually built up into the portrait of a city, a man, and – who could say? – perhaps a bit more. Their inspiration was openly acknowledged in the title, but it wasn't a question of imitation or parody, I explained to myself; it was more a question of trading on resonances, that most twentieth-century of techniques.

I continued my serendipitous drawings, which I thought could be used to illustrate *Spleenters*, if it ever got as far as publication (not that it needed to – having been written, it existed, whether discovered or not). I went to the most serious films I could find. Somehow, with Annick, we had often ended up finding common ground in an undemanding movie: a Western, an oldie, the latest Belmondo. Alone, it seemed, you could really get down to things: take notes of dialogue without being embarrassed; wander out of the cinema with the film still in your head, instead of having to find bright comments about it almost at once. I began to buy *Les Cahiers*.

I read; I began to cook, tentatively, a few French dishes; I hired a Solex for a week and put-putted off to Sceaux and Vincennes. I felt I was having a bloody good time; and whenever there was a knock on the door, my chest nearly fell inwards, and I wondered to myself, 'Annick?'

It never was. Once it was a neighbour asking if I had any Vittel as she'd forgotten it when she went shopping, and what with the stairs and her bones … Once it was Mme Huet, cross at having to come up to the third floor to fetch me, but it was the telephone, from England, and it might be urgent (someone might have died, she meant). When I got to the phone, my father told me he'd been hanging on for five minutes (Mme Huet had taken it punitively slowly up the stairs), and that the bill was going to be something frightful, but anyway, Happy Birthday. Ah; I'd completely forgotten.

And then, once, fairly late at night, a week before I was due to leave Paris, there was a different sort of knock. A tune in fact. Big knuckles rapping out the rhythm, finger-ends and background whistles harmonising and filling it out. After a brief panic at the thought of musical burglars, I recognised God Save the Queen; opened, and there were Mickey, Marion and Dave. Marion stood leaning against the banister, pretty, silent, and questioning. Mickey pulled out a comb wrapped in *papier de toilette* and gave me a burst of Auld Lang Syne. Dave had come as a parody Frog, in a blue-and-white horizontally striped jersey, beret, and a mean, corked-on moustache; he carried a *baguette* under his arm and was chewing garlic. The bread and the garlic hit me in different places as he stepped forward and kissed me on both cheeks.

'Bobbee Sharltong, Zhaqui Sharltong, Coupe du Monde, Monsieur 'Eat, God Shave the Queen.'

Mickey wound his way to the end of his tune. Marion smiled. I smiled. They didn't know what they'd done, but all was forgiven. We rolled into the flat and I took down a bottle of calvados to celebrate. Marion continued to watch and smile, while Dave and Mickey speculated.

'Pur'aps 'e 'as been malade.'

'Looks healthy enough to me. Perhaps he's been sulking.'

'Mais il n'est pas boudeur. Pur'aps 'e work 'ard.'

'Perhaps his doxy gave him the elbow.'

I glanced at Marion.

'Pur'aps zat yes,' said Dave. They gave me a chorus of Chevalier in Sank 'Eaven, with Dave violinning his *baguette*.

I smiled a sort of agreement.

Marion smiled back.

6 · Object Relations

Billancourt and the Bourse: what do they matter now? Ask me what I did in 1968 and I'll tell you: worked on my thesis (discovering a little-known exchange of letters between Hugo and Coleridge on the nature of poetic drama, which I published in the *Modern Language Quarterly*); fell in love, had my heart chipped; improved my French; wrote a lapidary volume, issued in a handwritten edition of one; did some drawing; made some friends; met my wife.

If I'd read that before leaving England, I'd have been scared stiff. Scared, impressed, yet also, perhaps, a little disappointed. All that stuff about a man's reach and grasp is true, of course; but maybe I'd set off with even grander expectations. What had I been after? For a start, a vivid, explosive, enriching self-knowledge. And then, I also dreamed about finding the key to some vital synthesis of art and life. How naïve it sounds, put like that. Still, the larger the question, the more naïve it always sounds. It was the only subject I'd been seriously interested in, from my early experiments with Toni in the National Gallery. 'Some people say that life is the thing, but I prefer reading': we would have endorsed that guiltily at the time, guilty because we feared that our passion for art was the result of the emptiness of our 'lives'. How did the two concepts interact? Where was the point of balance? Were they as distinguishable as we assumed them to be? Could a life be a work of art; or a work of art a higher form of life? Was art merely posh entertainment, on to which a fake spiritual side had been foisted by the non-religious? Life ended; but didn't art end too?

I sat in the creaky cane chair, waiting for it to be time to leave. Better half an hour here and half at the Gare du Nord than a whole hour at either place, giving loneliness and inactivity a chance to nest in the brain. Keep on the move or, next best thing, break up not being on the move.

My two suitcases, the weight evenly distributed between them, stood neatly side by side near the door. I took a last look round, saddened, but also vaguely proud that I was saddened. It was all experience, wasn't it? It was all living, wasn't it? Wasn't it?

To the left the bed where, as I still tenderly expressed it to myself, I had lost my virginity. I mentally put my arm round my own shoulder for a second; then shrugged it off. Annick, on the bed, acted, reacted, demanded, accused, forgave, disappeared. We could, of course, still be friends. I hadn't seen her for over a month.

A row of books I was leaving behind: mostly *Livres de Poche*, so vigorously read that the cellophane coverings had sprung away from the bullied, concave spines. Above them, a daub by the flat's owner, early Cubist colours dashed on with the glee of Derain. Not a great success, I thought for the last time, and smiled at the parting gift I had left on the table: loyally neat drawing of the view from the window, every coping-stone etched in, every television aerial identifiable, every parked car included – the result a curious monochrome mixture of clarity and bustle. I was modestly very impressed by it.

The fruit machine, with the pile of old francs on the shelf above it. A miraculous, ironic instrument: you put things into it and then, at seeming random, but actually according to a programme, you got things back. You thought you profited but in fact you didn't, though if you went on long enough you might end up not making a loss. On top of which, what you actually put in and got out had no current value! Worn-out museum-pieces, trite copper circles. If you were feeling self-indulgent, the machine offered itself as a gloomy enough symbol.

My cases, mockingly well-aligned, packed in response to no humid *brise marine*.

The door, through which Annick had come. Through which I still wanted her to return? Through which she would, had she known, still have come?

On the desk, a line-up of bottles of spirits, one for each calvados I'd consumed. Beside it, a wastepaper basket which I had, with deliberate negligence, failed to empty; though I hadn't actually planted evidence, I was certainly conscious of what was in it. A copy of *Hara-Kiri* (*'journal bête et méchant'*) and one of *Les Nouvelles Littéraires*; a theatre programme which happened to be a duplicate; various rough drafts of stories and poems; a few drawings (the best rejects); a couple of letters from my parents; some tangerine peel; and a note from Annick, left one morning when she had gone off early. *'Pas mal, mon vieux, t'es pas mal du tout. A demain. A.'* That too was practically a duplicate.

The final object was me. Packed tight like my suitcase – I'd had to sit on top of me to get it all in. The moral and sensual equivalents of theatre programmes were all there, bundled up chronologically and bound with rubber bands. Look, it all happened, they said, as I riffled through them again. Look at this, and this, and this. See how you reacted here, and here. Wasn't that a bit shitty? And Christ, look at this, now if you don't feel ashamed about this, I give up on you. You do feel ashamed? That's the ticket. OK, now you can look at this one – you didn't do at all badly here; genuine sensitivity I'd say, compassion, even (though it's jumping the gun a bit to mention the word) wisdom. Instinctive wisdom, perhaps, rather than the long-learnt sort; but not to be despised for all that.

I patted it all back into place, tightened the straps, got up from the chair with a final creak, gathered my external suitcases, and left. In my pocket was the book I'd just started: *L'Education Sentimentale*.

PART THREE
Metroland II (1977)

Things and actions are what they are, and the consequences of them will be what they will be; why then should we desire to be deceived?

Bishop Butler

I suppose I must be grown-up now. Or would 'adult' be a better word, a more ... adult word? If you came and inventoried me, I'd have ticks in all the appropriate boxes. I'm surprised how well camouflaged I seem. Age: Thirty/Married: Yes/ Children: One/Job: One/House: Yes/With mortgage: Yes/ (Rock solid so far)/Car: Arguable/Jury Service: Once, finding accused not guilty after long discussion of 'reasonable doubt'/ Pets: No, because they mess up/Foreign holidays: Yes/ Prospects: Bloody better be/Happiness: Oh, yes; and if not now, then never.

I make such lists in my head on the odd night when sleep fails and panic gusts across my mind. Sometimes, the categories can be different, though: more aggressive and muscular, picked to see off the shifting fears of the night. Healthy, white, British, recently made love, not poor, not deformed, not starving, not hounded by religion, not made paranoid by nerves or emotions. It's odd how the list slopes off into negatives; but negatives provide adequate comfort if you're already in bed next to your wife, while downstairs, mutedly, reassuringly, the refrigerator changes gear. I find myself relieved again, content to be within my own skin.

Adult, yes, that's an overall comfort too. At least, I conclude I must be. A few years ago I used to worry about it in a straining sort of way. Why haven't I spotted some signal changing to green, some notice being held up from the pits, some celestial nod (not too public) letting me know I'm there? This feeling began to pass, however; largely because nobody ever challenged me. Nobody came up and said, You shirked that tackle, *ergo* you aren't a man, go back and start again with a new set of principles and handicaps. I used to think this was about to happen, and would come over shifty; but people are amiable. At times, I suspect that the concept of maturity is maintained by a conspiracy of niceness.

And there are other ways to calm nocturnal fears. Sometimes, lying awake, while out there in the darkness a new date clicks into place, I turn towards Marion, dog-legged beside me, and head off down the bed. Upside down like a duck, I stealthily work away at her nightdress, which tangles round her legs as she twists herself off into sleep. The trick (does Marion silently connive?) is for me to take possession of her, and then gradually wake her with something stronger than a kiss. This time, she stirs more reluctantly than usual.

'Whozzat?'

'Three guesses,' I ho-ho.

'Nnn.'

'NNNNNNNNN.'

'What day is it, Chris?'

'Sunday.'

'Quite tired.'

'Ah, well, I didn't mean Sunday/Monday, love. It's, er, Saturday/Sunday. About, a bit after twelve. Double O thirty in fact.'

This pedantic foreplay makes us giggle gently.

'Nnn.'

She parts her thighs loosely, reaches between them with her free hand, and pulls at me. Conversation ceases. We go off into noises.

Afterwards (that still stretchy word) we subside away from each other, drowsy, feeling as if we had shares in everything. I think these times must be the happiest of my life. People say that happiness is boring; not for me. They also say that all happy people are happy in the same way. Who cares; in any case, at times like this I'm hardly interested in arguing the toss.

1 · Nude, Giant Girls

When do the theories stop? And why? Say what you will, they stop for most of us. Are they killed by a single decisive event? For some, perhaps. But usually, they die by attrition; lingeringly, circumstantially. And afterwards you wonder: how seriously did we mean them anyway?

On Sunday mornings I slip out of the house early. I turn left, past sensible detached houses: Ravenshoe, with its scatter of horse-chestnut flowers on the pavement; Vue de Provence, with its green shutters; East Coker, with a smirk-provoking carport. They have their names carved in Gothic letters on slices of wood which are screwed to trees.

I pick my way across the golf course, watching an early drive catch the dew on its first bounce and pull up quickly, glistening. I like it here; I like the misty, different perspective. From high up by the fourth tee, you can follow tiny figures pulling trolleys along the fairway, and bursting into striped colour at the touch of rain. From here, the self-condemning cries of 'Fo-o-o-ore' seem distant and comic (I smile as I remember Toni's answering bellow of 'Ski-i-i-in'). Below, smart silver trains process, with the clack of muted knitting machines; their windows flash the sun at you, like boys with playground mirrors. Churches remind other people to get up and pray.

It's certainly ironic to be back in Metroland. As a boy, what would I have called it: *le syphilis de l'âme*, or something like that, I dare say. But isn't part of growing up being able to ride irony without being thrown? Besides, it's an efficient place to live. Next to the record shop is a grocer's which sells eggs with shit and straw on them; two minutes' walk from where Marion gets her hair done you can see real pigs mucking up a field. Five minutes' drive and you're in open country where only the pylons remind you of town life. As a boy, when we drove past these pylons, I would elbow Nigel out of his SF magazine with a whisper of 'Look, nude, giant girls'. Nowadays, when we pass them, I still think of the poem, but find it excited and inexact.

When do the theories stop? I remember suddenly, from my early times with Marion, a drive we took one cold December night. We ended up in a cinema car park, left the heater on, and talked. We talked so much in that Morris Minor convertible of hers that I can still read off to myself the dashboard controls from left to right.

'So?' It was the way Marion always started our chats; it was her first word after the sliding clatter of the handbrake.

'So? Still love you.'

'Ah. Good.' A kiss; another; a browse in the down of her cheek.

'As I did yesterday.'

'Good. So?' Her chin seemed firmly set, I noticed; it wasn't just the polo-neck sweater that made it jut.

'Not enough for you?'

'Probably enough for me. Not enough for you.'

' ... ?'

'And therefore, eventually, not enough for me either.'

'Shee-it. Is this Le Petit Coq all over again?' That had been the Paris café where we'd first sensed – and I'd almost feared – our interest in each other.

' ... '

'What do you want me to say?' I genuinely wanted to know; almost.

'Well, I don't just want you to say something you think I want to hear.' (Fair enough, but why didn't things get easier? I thought the more you loved someone, the easier things became. There were just as many traps as ever.)

'Is it *that* question?' The question that came from all those different angles.

'I want to feel you're thinking about it.'

'I'll think about it. Will you marry me?'

'I'll think about it.'

'I'd like to think you were thinking about it.'

We talked and kissed on. The cinema-goers drove off and emptied the park. We couldn't start the car: the heater had run the battery flat. Eventually an AA man arrived, noted the steamed-up windows, and commented chidingly, 'Just a case of over-heating, sir and madam.'

Toni didn't come to the wedding. I had a letter explaining that he felt unable on principle to attend. That's what his first line said, anyway; I didn't bother to read on, and threw the letter away. Two days later he rang up.

'Well?'

'Well what?'

'Good letter?'

'I didn't read it.'

'Fuck, why not? I mean, if you aren't interested in reading a carefully argued case against marriage now, then when are you?'

'Well, the funny thing is I *do* seem rather less interested now than on other occasions. Were you going for an épat or something?'

'Shit, no, we've grown out of that, haven't we? No, I just thought you'd appreciate a certain historical overview of your contemplated action.'

'Toni, how thoughtful.'

'Don't get me wrong. I mean, I quite like Marion, you know. Not my type, of course ... '

'Well that's a relief—though I suppose historical circumstances might have prevented you taking her off my hands?'

'I don't follow you.'

'Then fuck off, Toni.'

'I really don't see what you're getting worked up about.'

'Well, one of us is thick, then.'

'Anyway, it's interesting, you know – I looked up *mariage* the other day in the Frog dic. Did you know that all the phrases in which it's used are disparaging: *mariage de convenance, d'intérêt, blanc, de raison, à la mode* ... and so on.'

'*Mariage d'inclination*?'

'Missed it.'

'I haven't' – and I put the phone down.

And then I remember an overcast morning six years ago. 11.30. I was on the pavement outside Kennington Register Office with a small, sharp pain in my back and a large, indistinct one in my stomach. Marion and I were standing side by side trying to keep plausible smiles on our faces while squinting anxiously around to see if anyone had disobediently brought confetti. Friends with cameras kept trying to clown us into ridiculous poses. Marion did a fake-pregnancy shot, turning her feet out, leaning back, and acting nausea. Someone (Dave, I think) had brought along an antique shotgun, and we tried to persuade passers-by of the right age to pose pointing it at me. The trouble was, no one who looked respectable enough to be Marion's father would agree to the sacrilege asked of them. Eventually, a semi-tramp pushing his possessions in a super-market trolley came past, and we got him to stand with his back to the camera and aim the weapon at me. Afterwards, we had to wrestle the gun back off him, since he seemed to regard it as his fee.

When we got back to Marion's flat to change for the recep-tion (the bargain with our parents had been a 'proper' reception in exchange for a ceremony on our own terms), I discovered the source of the pain in my back: I'd missed a packing pin when climbing into my new white shirt. As for the other pain, the roaming, restless one in my belly, I wondered, as I glanced across at Marion's gentle, sweet, strong, happy, lovable face, if it was fear.

Marion found me my first real job. I was supply teaching in Wandsworth at the time: twenty-five quid a week for the privilege of having your bicycle tyres let down each week by different kids at different schools, and of being asked by muscled fifteen-year-olds if you were queer. Even the weight of Toni's approval (he liked people to have jobs they hated: called it 'social yeast') couldn't alleviate my angry boredom. Fortunately Marion would come over to see me in my septic bedsitter; and I would lie staring up through the veil of her hair at the damp-stains on the ceiling.

One day she was leafing through a pile of careers-board handouts and read: 'Ewart Porter require trainee copywriter: £1,650 p.a., increments assessed every six months. Lively, adaptable ... ' and all the usual bromides.

'Not exactly what I had in mind.'

'Is here what you had in mind?'

To my surprise they took me on. To my further surprise, I enjoyed the job. Toni's scorn was neutralised by Marion's approval; also, it never felt like work. It was like being paid for playing sport, or doing crosswords; you even became exhilarated and competitive during big campaigns. I remember helping launch a new cooking fat called Lift, which duly justified our office joke and never got off the ground. We all felt we had to beat the rival cooking-fat slogans – 'It's as easy as Spry' was one motto held up to us as a paragon of memor-ability. We toiled away at 'Give your cooking Lift-off' (astro-naut with fluffy cakes), 'Going up? Take a Lift' (bellboy with fluffy cakes), and even – for a special offer – 'Don't look a Lift-horse in the mouth' (frisky colt with fluffy cakes). It was ridiculous, but pleasant. Besides, I never saw it as a dangerous career. There were poets and novelists in advertising, they said; though I could never quite remember their names when asked. I did know that Eliot had worked in a bank.

Three years later, through Dave, I moved to Harlow Tewson. They'd only been in business a short while, but already their catchily designed reference books were in every cork-tiled kitchen, pine-panelled bathroom and gaudy Renault 4. I've been an editor there for five years, with no regrets. It also doesn't make me feel shitty: we don't fight against making money, but we use good people, and we produce good books. At the moment, for instance, I'm working on a book about Italian Renaissance painting: a TV tie-in to go with a series of drama-documentaries based on Vasari. Toni – who objects to the idea that artists have lives as well as works – has already thought up our chapter titles for us: Buonarotti Bangs. Leo gets Lucky. Sandro Screws. Masaccio – and so on. There's always a lot of so on with Toni.

'What do you do on your walks, Chris?'

(Once I would have responded, not dishonestly, but with a little deviousness: 'Toning up the muscles for your delectation', or something like that. But I've given up – I think – half-truths, just as I've given up meta-communication: wonderful in theory, but unreliable in practice.)

'Oh, well, I suppose I think a bit.'

'What about?' She seemed sweetly troubled, as if she ought to be doing the same and hadn't found time for it.

'Oh, serious shit mostly.'

' ... ?'

'Stuff. Past – future; stuff. Secular confession, some of it. I pray, love and remember.'

Again, a troubled smile. She came across and kissed me. I took her to be meta-communicating the fact that she wanted to kiss me (and for once let myself off checking up).

'Love you,' she said, breathing into my shoulder.

'Love you back.'

'Good.'

'And you front.'

Marion giggled. In marriage, they say, all bad jokes are good jokes.

Another comforting list I make is the list of reasons why I married Marion.

Because I loved her of course.

Why to that, then.

Because she was (is) sensible, intelligent, pretty.

Because she didn't use love as a way of finding out about the world: didn't look on the other person (I suppose I mean me) as a means of obtaining information.

Because she didn't sleep with me straight away, but didn't hold out with reckless principle; and afterwards showed no remorse.

Because deep down, I sometimes think, I fear her a little.

Because I once asked her, 'Will you love me regardless of what happens?' and she replied, 'You must be off your head.'

Because she was the only child of comfortably-off parents. Money may not be the fuel of love, Auden said, but it makes excellent kindling.

Because she tolerates my making restless lists like this.

Because she loves me.

Because if it's true, as Maugham observed, that the tragedy of life is not that men die, but that they cease to love, then Marion is a person with whom even falling out of love would have its compensations.

Because I have said that I love her, and there is no turning back. No cynicism is intended. The orthodoxy runs, that if a marriage is founded on less than perfect truth it will always come to light. I don't believe that. Marriage moves you further away from the examination of truth, not nearer to it. No cynicism is intended there either.

2 · Running Costs

I don't see so much of Toni nowadays. We're still nostalgic about each other, but realise that our paths have diverged. After Morocco, he went off to the States for a couple of years (from kif to kitsch as he put it); he came back, taught philosophy, and established himself as a callous academic reviewer; he published poems and two books of essays, and gradually become more involved in street politics. He lives now with a girl whose name we can never remember in the least fashionable part of the borough of Kensington he could find. The last time we asked him down we invited his 'wife' as well; but he said he'd come alone.

'I'm sorry is it Kelly couldn't come,' said Marion as we were sitting down over an aperitif.

'Kally. No, well, we believe in having separate friends you see.'

'You mean that you didn't want her to meet us? Or that she didn't want to come? Which?'

Toni looked a bit surprised. I think he thinks of Marion as unassertive because she's quiet.

'No, she'd probably like meeting you. We just have separate friends.'

'Did you ... tell her she was invited?'

'Uh, mattrafact no.'

'So we don't get any choice about meeting her either?'

'Don't get heavy, Marion.' (He pronounced it to rhyme with Carry On) 'The situation's quite clear isn't it?'

'Quite clear. I'd better get back to the lunch.'

It was a bit embarrassing; I always forget between meetings how contrary Toni has remained. But then, you only have to look at us to see the ways we are going. I had on a crew-neck sweater, corduroy trousers and Hush Puppies. Toni wore couture jeans, a denim waistcoat, an ingeniously rumpled shirt, and a sort of stalker's anorak; his hair was lacquered by neglect; and his battered shoulder bag contained, I imagine, lots of things I never needed. He still looked as swarthy and Jewish and energetic and two-shaves-a-day as ever; though I noticed he had lately taken to plucking the area where his eyebrows had once joined hands. He also seemed to talk a little differently from how I'd remembered: the accent was the same, but grammar and vocabulary had taken on a more demotic cast.

I'd expected Toni to be combative – we'd both been so at school. I just hadn't thought he would make such a big point out of a simple invitation. After some edgy conversation we sat down to lunch. Amy was perched in her high chair on Toni's left, her yellow Pelican bib fastened round her neck. Immediately he made a great play of putting his anorak on and moving his place-setting a few inches to the right out of what he called chucking-range.

'Never know when they're going to chuck, you know,' he told us with all the authority of a non-parent. He didn't mean throw either.

'She's very good,' Marion said firmly. 'Aren't you, pet? Except when she's got bad wind, of course.'

Toni pretended to quail. 'Why is a normal baby like an unsuccessful crap?' Marion frowned a little; I said I didn't know. 'Because they're both all piss and wind.' Marion passed him some soup without comment. Toni took the opportunity of moving a few more inches along the table. 'No, you never can tell, you see. That's why I always wear my baby clothes.' (He waved a sleeve of his anorak) 'Wear them for babies, slumming and gardening. Oh, and getting money out of the Arts Council.'

'We qualify under the second as well as the first, I take it?' asked Marion, understandably irritated.

'Natch.' Toni turned towards Amy and pulled his mouth into a clown's grin. 'Chuck, chuck, chuck,' he gurgled in a rough parody of a doting uncle. 'There's a good little chucker. Just a little chuck for Toni.' He held out one sleeve invitingly.

'Very good indeed, love,' I intervened, less than comfortably, waving my spoon over the watercress soup. Marion waited for Toni's confirmation of the assessment; but he was too busy stuffing his mouth with bread.

'Tell us about *you*, Toni,' she said after a pause.

'Ah; having a vasectomy – got to cut down running costs somehow. Writing for the Theatre-on-Wheels. Trying to get the local Labour fascists to haul ass. Doing some research for *Koestler – A Study in Duplicity*. Sponging meals off old schoolfriends.'

'And their wives,' Marion corrected.

'And their delightfully ironic if somewhat tart wives.'

At that moment, a sort of whoop came from Amy. She coughed, and then started to be gently sick; a milky stream ran down into her plastic catcher. Toni laughed his triumph. Amy gurgled at him in reply. He pretended to swab down his anorak, and we all relaxed. Once we adjusted to his apparent rudeness and solipsism we got on well enough. Marion once complained that she found Toni insensitive. I said it was more a case of a writer simply telling the truth as he saw it all the time. 'I thought writers were meant to be more not less sensitive than other people,' she'd answered. There's a difference between sensitivity and politeness, I think I said; and can't remember whether I convinced myself.

After lunch, Toni and I went round the garden. He ignored the 'escapist' flowers, and cross-questioned me on the soil, the varieties of vegetable, the likely yield. The year he had spent on a co-operative farming venture in Wales seemed to have left him with some empirical knowledge, but little understanding of horticultural principle.

'So this is it, eh?' he asked me with an undermining smile as we stared creatively at a row of swede. 'So this is it?'

I thought I'd duck that one until its thrust became clearer, so I answered with another question.

'You're much more ... political than you used to be, aren't you?'

'I'm more left-wing, if that's what you mean. Man is never not political.'

'Come on. We were totally passive about it as adolescents. Totally scornful and uninterested, don't you remember? It was art that counted wasn't it? *We* are the movers and shakers, don't you remember that *we* emphasis?'

'I remember that we were totally Tory.'

'I don't think that's right at all. We hated the fat cats, didn't we? And the *bon bourgeois*? "*Le Belge est voleur* ... " ' I began, but couldn't remember the rest of it.

'We had apathy and distaste, I agree, but they're fundamental planks of the Tory platform, aren't they? Christ, don't you remember Cuba? What were we doing — cheering on Kennedy as if he were Robert Ryan in *The Battle of the Bulge*,' (wasn't that right?) 'And what did we think about Profumo? Mainly envy: that was the result of our analysis of the socio-political crisis.'

'But *poetry* makes nothing happen,' I said with a reasonable-man cadence.

'Too fucking right. So if you want to make things happen, don't write poetry. I don't know why I do; change from wanking, I suppose. Picked up a book of poems in Dillon's the other day, didn't get past the preface — it said "This book was written to change the world". Too fucking ironic for words.'

'Why get so heated?'

'Because the *reason* poetry makes nothing happen is because those same old fat cats won't let it.'

'Who won't let it? Which fat cats? Come on, be precise.'

'Imprecise fucking fat cats. Movable fat cats. Because poetry's packaged as a late-night slot, a quite minority taste unquote, like water-skiing or goat-fucking or something. Who reads it? Who's been told it counts?'

'There's a lot of poetry in the papers.'

'Ha – the more, the less. That's just fucking infill. They ring up some tame cunt and say, "Oh Jonathan, can we have a four-by-two this week?" or "I'm afraid our ballet critic's sprained his wrist doing capital letters, could we have something long with short lines? Rhymes, please, you know our readers like rhymes." '

'I don't thing that's very fair.' (Frankly, I thought it was paranoid, the crabby disenchantment of an unsuccessful writer.)

' 'Course it's not *fair*.' (Toni pronounced 'fair' with the sarcasm he normally reserved for 'Tory') 'But it's the way it works. Ask for poetry in a shop and you get jolly ballads or dead cunts' stuff. What's it to do with now? Same with novels: it's all smugglers and asshole rabbits and *history*.'

'And we all know what history is,' I cued nostalgically (better get him off this, I thought).

'The lays of the victors. Quite. But why doesn't anyone take books seriously any more? I mean, apart from academics, and what the fuck good are they – they're only reviewers delivering their copy a hundred years late. Why does everyone sneer when a writer makes a political statement? Why does anything left-wing have to be trendy before it's read, and by the time it's trendy it's already a force for conservatism? And why the *fuck*' (he seemed to be drawing breath at long last) 'why the *fuck* don't people buy my fucking books?'

'Too dirty?' I suggested. He laughed, began to calm down, and started awarding marks to the garden again.

'And why haven't you done anything, you budding fat cat?'

I didn't tell him about my projected history of transport around London.

'Oh, me, gee, shucks, I'm into life.'

He laughed again, though quite sympathetically, or so it seemed to me.

(But isn't it true that I'm – not 'into life', I wouldn't put it like that – I'm more serious? At school I would have called myself serious, whereas I was merely intense. In Paris I did call myself serious – imagined, indeed, that I was heading for some grand synthesis of life and art – but I was probably only attaching an inordinate, legitimating importance to unreflecting pleasure. Nowadays I'm serious about different things; and I don't fear my seriousness will collapse beneath me.)

'You mean you don't live in a rented room any more,' was Toni's comment when I paraphrased this to him. We were now at the bottom of the garden; looking through the trellis of bean-rods you could just make out the dormer window at the top of the house: one day, it would be Amy's room, or perhaps Amy's brother's.

'Well, up to a point. It's satisfying knowing your roof doesn't leak.'

'Caveman,' murmured Toni in one of our school accents.

'And in having your family huddled round you under your protection.'

'Chauvinist.'

'And actually, you know, in having a child.' (I wouldn't normally have mentioned this, because Toni's 'wife' had recently had what Toni called a Hoover-job; yet I felt under unfair attack.)

'But I thought it was a mistake.'

'She wasn't exactly planned, no; but I don't see that that makes any difference.'

'Well, I just think it's an odd formula: get the London Rubber Company to put pinpricks in the end of every Durex, and we get a new maturity in our population: serious-minded, caring, mortgaged up to their balls. They might even start buying my fucking books.'

We walked on, and stopped by the dwarf peas.

'By the way,' he said, working his elbow up and down in a licentious gesture from the past, 'had a bit on the side yet?'

My first instinct was to tell him to mind his own sodding business. My second was to ignore the question. My third (why does it take so long?) was to say simply,

'No.'

'That's interesting.'

'Why is No interesting?' (What did he have to be superior about?) 'You mean how amazing that I've been faithful for six years? That you wouldn't have lasted a week?'

'No, what's interesting is the pause before the No. Is it – No but I wouldn't half mind a bit? No but I nearly got some last week? No because Marion shags me out too much?'

'Actually, it was: Shall I smash his face in – No, on second thoughts I'll tell him the truth. I take it you and Kally have some modern arrangement?'

'Modern, old, don't mind what you call it – anything except your soiled old Judaeo-Christian rubbish topped up with Victorian wankers' sex-hatred.' He stared at me belligerently.

'But I'm not Jewish, I don't go to church, I don't wank – I merely love my wife.'

'That's what they all say. And you can still go on saying it when you've had the other. I take it you do still believe that when you die, you die?'

'Of course.'

'Well, that's a relief. Then how the fuck can you bear to think that until you die you'll never fuck another woman? How can you bear it? I'd just go mad. I mean, I'm sure Marion's terrific and all that and puts her heels in your ears and drains you as dry as a loofah, but even so ... '

I wanted to end the conversation, but the image he had produced of Marion was so suddenly, so oddly hurtful (keep your filthy thoughts off my wife); besides, who did he think he was to lecture me?

'Well, I'm not going into the details you'd doubtless enjoy, but our sex life' (I paused, already feeling almost disloyal) 'has, well quite enough variety ... '

Toni worked his elbow up and down again.

'You don't mean ... '

I had to head this one off quickly: 'Look, just because you live on the Metropolitan Line, it doesn't mean you haven't heard of ... ' I felt angry, then suddenly prim, and couldn't finish my sentence. I felt assailed by the images I had started up of my own accord.

'Careful where you put your tongue,' said Toni delightedly. 'Careless talk costs wives.'

'And as for not ... sleeping with anyone else, I don't see it how you see it. I don't spend my whole time in bed with Marion thinking, "I hope I don't die before I've had it away with somebody else". And anyway, once you're used to ... caviare you don't get an urge for ... boiled cod.'

'There are more fish in the sea than that. Fish, fish, fish.' Toni didn't go on, waited smiling, inviting me to continue. I was irritated, as much at my awkward choice of metaphor as anything.

'And anyway, I don't believe in this new orthodoxy. It used to be, don't screw around because you'll be unhappy and catch VD and give it to your wife and have mad children, like in Strindberg or Ibsen or whoever it was. Now it's screw around otherwise you'll become a bore and won't meet new people and will eventually become impotent with everyone except your wife.'

'Which isn't true?'

'Of course it isn't true; it's just fashionable prejudice.'

'Then why does it upset you? Why get so agitated when you defend what you believe in?'

'Because people like you keep nagging people like me and writing books about it. Do you remember, when we were kids, someone came up with the theory of the Adulterous Prop? I'm not saying, in some cases, it isn't a valid idea. It's just that nowadays what you get is a bloody great set of scaffolding.'

Toni paused; I could sense the counter-attack coming.

'So you're not a faithful husband because of, say, God's command?'

'Of course not.'

'Perhaps because of a categorical imperative: Screw not, lest thy wife be screwn?'

'No, I'm not possessive in that way.'

'Maybe it's not a question of principle with you at all?'

I felt apprehensive, as if I were being guided towards a sheep-dip and didn't know what was going to be in it. Acid, no doubt, knowing Toni. He went on,

'Have you ever discussed it with Marion?'

'No.'

'Why not? I thought it was the first thing couples discussed.'

'Well, to be quite honest, I have thought of mentioning it once or twice, but I don't see how you can bring it up without making the other person think that there's something behind it all.'

'Or rather someone.'

'If you like.'

'So you don't know whether she'd mind or not?'

'I'm sure she'd mind. Just as I'd mind the other way round.'

'But she hasn't asked you either?'

'No, I said not.'

'So it's just … '

' … a feeling. But a strong one. I know it; I feel it.'

Toni sighed, with unnecessary breathiness; here comes the sheep-dip, I thought.

'What is it,' (trying to redirect him) 'aren't I interested enough in adultery for you?'

'No, I was just thinking how things change. Do you remember, when we were at school, when life had a capital letter and it was all Out There somehow, we used to think that the way to live our lives was to discover or deduce certain principles from which individual decisions could be worked out? Seemed obvious to everyone but wankers at the time, didn't it? Remember reading all those late Tolstoy pamphlets called things like *The Way We Ought To Live*? I was just wondering really if you would have despised yourself then if you'd known you were going to end up making decisions based on hunches which you could easily verify, but couldn't be bothered to? I mean, I don't think I find it particularly surprising; I just find it depressing.'

There was a long silence during which we didn't look at each other. I had the feeling that this time *esprit de l'escalier* was going to take even longer to come than normal. Toni eventually continued:

'I mean, perhaps I'm just as bad. I suppose I make lots of

decisions on grounds of selfishness which I call pragmatism. I suppose in a way that's just as bad as you.'

It was as if, having drowned me, he had stood around waiting for the body to be washed up, and then offered it some half-hearted artificial respiration.

We walked back to the house, and I told him a lot about plants on the way.

3 · Stiff Petticoat

The irony was that while I was being dressed down by Toni I could have said more; a little more, anyway. But maybe there's a pleasure in knowing that you're being wrongly assessed.

Can you confess to virtue? I don't know, but I'll give it a try. It's a shady enough concept nowadays, after all. Perhaps virtue sounds too strong a word, though, implies something too positive. Or perhaps not. Who am I to shrug off a compliment? If you can commit a crime by failing to pull a drowning man out of a pond, then why can't you be called virtuous for resisting temptation?

It began with a chance encounter on the 5.45 from Baker Street. I was waiting for it to pull out when a briefcase raked my ribs. I shifted sideways to allow room for the sort of slack-thighed fatty that the line caters for, when I heard,

'Lloyd. It is Lloyd, isn't it?' I turned.

'Penny.' I knew he was Tim; he knew I was Chris; but even during the season when, as quail-boned twelve-year-olds, we'd played left and right centre together in a house rugger team, we'd never ventured beyond surnames. Later, he'd gone into the Maths sixth and become a prefect: membership of two despised classes had made him no longer acceptable company, merely a person to be nodded at in corridors while Toni and I loudly discussed the dynamic ambiguity of Hopkins.

He still looked chunky, curly-haired and prefectorial; his commuter's rig hardly changed him at all. I knew he'd gone up to Cambridge on a Shell scholarship: £700 a year in exchange for three years of his post-graduate life (usual bit of boss-class strong-arming, Toni and I had thought). As the train bored its way to Finchley Road, he filled me in on the rest: met his geography-teaching wife at – of all unpleasant ideas – a pyjama party; stayed with Shell for five years, then went to Unilever; three kids, two cars; struggling to pay for private education – the usual tale of banal prosperity.

'Photographs?' I asked, pretty bored.

'What do you mean, photographs?'

'Wife and kids – don't you carry them around?'

'I only see them every day and all weekend – why the hell should I carry their photos around?'

I had to smile. I stared out of the window at a new tower-block hospital on the edge of playing fields: from high above, the football nets looked the size of hockey goals, the hockey goals like water-polo nets. An early-evening mist hung here and there at ankle height. I began to swap my life for his. Maybe it was guilt at having offended him, or maybe it was the truth, but my life, as it came out that evening, sounded rather like his, except for a lower fertility rate.

Once I'd discarded my instinctive responses, I found that we got on well enough. I told him I was thinking of writing a social history of travel round London.

'Bloody interesting,' he said, and I couldn't help feeling pleased. 'Always wanted to know about that sort of stuff. Actually, I saw Dicky Simmons the other day – you remember him – and for some reason we got talking about all the disused tunnels there must be under London. Railway tunnels, post-office tunnels. He knows about things like that – works for the GLC now. Might be useful to you.'

He might indeed. Simmons had been an embarrassing schoolboy: lonely, unpredictable, dandruffy, lacking in confidence. He didn't look right either: and the regulation short haircut had only emphasised the ostentatious discord of his features. He spent his lunchtimes lurking in a corner of the sixth-form balcony, his bony, much-picked nose aimed at an obscure work of sexology, while with his free hand he tried pathetically to flatten back to his head a ninety-degree ear. There had been no hope, then, for Simmons.

'Don't jump,' said Tim, 'but Dicky and I are going to the OBA's annual dinner next month. Come along and meet him.'

I ruefully promised to bear it in mind. In the meantime, he asked Marion and me to 'a little cheese-and-wine do' the following Saturday. I said we'd come as long as we didn't have to wear pyjamas.

In the event, we couldn't get a baby-sitter, so I went alone. The plot was trite: husband alone at party for the first time in years – drink in pipkinfuls – girl in Fifties revival clothes and lipstick (nostalgic, fetishist effect on husband) – talk of this and that and also of the other – both giggle-drunk – some flirting, verbal feel-up. And then, suddenly, it all started to go wrong; wrong, that is, in terms of my mild fantasy.

'OK then?' she suddenly said.

'OK what?' I replied. She looked at me for a few seconds, then said, in a threateningly sober tone.

'OK so we go and fuck?' (How old was she, for Christ's sake: twenty? twenty-one?)

'Oh well, I don't know about *that*,' I answered, suddenly a blushing fifteen, holding down my stiff petticoat.

'Why not? Afraid to put your cock where your mouth is?' She suddenly leaned forward and kissed me on the lips.

I hadn't felt this sort of panic for years. I thought, I hope to God it's that new sort of lipstick which doesn't come off on you. I looked around the room to see if anyone had noticed. I couldn't see that anyone had. Then I looked again, seeking to catch someone's eye, anyone's. I couldn't. Instead, I dropped my voice and said firmly,

'I'm married.'

'I'm not prejudiced.'

The odd thing was, it didn't feel like a tricky moral situation at all (maybe that was because I only half fancied her); just a tricky social situation. I recovered some of my nerve.

'I'm glad to hear it. But you see, "I'm married" was short-hand.'

'It usually is. Which one is it this time – I'll fuck you but don't want to get involved; or I'll fuck you and am interested but think we ought to get it all out in the open first; or My wife doesn't understand me and I don't know whether to fuck you or not but maybe we could just go somewhere and talk; or is it just plain I'm not going to fuck you?'

'If those are the only available categories, then it's the last.'

'In that case' – she leaned towards me, and I half-ducked to one side – 'you shouldn't tease cunt.' Christ. Her detached zest was turning to aggression. Is that how they all talk nowadays? Ten years suddenly felt a long time. I thought, Stop, *I'm* the one who's meant to be in his prime; *I'm* the one who's experienced yet not set in his ways, principled yet flexible. That's *me*.

'Don't be ridiculous.'

'Well you wouldn't deny that you were – how would you put it? – leading me on?'

'Umm, no more than you were me.' (You couldn't compliment a girl these days without being sued for breach of promise.)

'But I was trying to get off with you, wasn't I?'

'I admit I was ... flirting with you.'

'Well, then, you're a cunt-teaser, aren't you?' and she repeated, in the clipped, condescending tone of one instructing a child, 'Don't tease cunt.'

The odd thing was, I still found her rather attractive (though her features seemed to have become a little sharper by association); I still wanted to charm her in some way.

'But why is everything so prescriptive and indivisible? Don't you ever want to listen to just one track of a record? If you ... I don't know ... open a packet of dates, do you have to scoff the lot?'

'Thanks for the comparisons. It's not a question of degree, just of honesty of intention. You were dishonest. You're ... '

'All right, all right,' (I didn't want to be held down by the neck with my nose in that word again) 'I admit a mild deception. But no more than if I'd asked you what job you did and you told me and I said "How interesting" even though I happened to think it the most boring job in the world. It's just a fact of social protocol.'

She looked at me with an expression poised between disbelief and contempt, then walked off. Why was I being accused of deviousness? I wondered, with a pained loyalty to myself. And why were there so many misunderstandings about sex?

Later, on the train home, I remembered Toni's Theory of Suburban Sex, which he had once elaborated to me when we were both sixteen and had yet to enter the land without signposts. London, he explained, was the centre of power and industry and money and culture and everything valuable, important and good; it was therefore, *ex hypothesi*, the centre of sex. Look at the number of gold-chained prostitutes for a start; and look at any Underground carriage – tight-clothed chippies all pressed up against Grosz caricatures. The closeness, the sweat, the urgency of the city all roared Sex at any observer of sensitivity. Now this sexual energy, he assured me, became gradually dissipated as you moved away from the metropolis, until, by the time you got to Hitchin and Wendover and Haywards Heath, people had to look up books to find out what went where. This explained the widespread sexual abuse of animals in the countryside – simple ignorance. You don't get animals being abused in the city.

But in the suburbs, Toni went on (he was probably helping me understand my parents at the time), you are in a strange intermediate area of sexual twilight. You might think of the suburbs – Metroland, for instance – as being erotically soporific; yet the grand itch animated the most unlikely people. You never knew where you were: a chippy might turn you down; a golfer's wife might rip off your school uniform without a by-your-leave and do gaudy, perverse things to you; shop assistants could jump either way. The Pope had formally banned nuns from living in the suburbs; Toni was quite confident of this. It was here, he maintained, that the really interesting bits of sex took place.

There might, I thought that evening, be something in the Theory after all.

4 · Is Sex Travel?

Marion and I hadn't seen Uncle Arthur for some months when Nigel rang to tell us he had died. I can't claim the family was plunged into black; surprise was the nearest thing to grief any of us could muster. The last fifteen years hadn't made me feel any more affectionate towards him; the most you could say was that I grew to respect the honesty of his dislike for me, and to value his warping self-sufficiency.

As Arthur grew older he became more transparently and more insultingly mendacious. In his prime, his ploys had always been carefully prepared: the frangibility of his spinal cord or the old-soldier stiffness of his knee would be established early on: from his sincere glare you suspected he might be lying about them, but couldn't be sure. Only later would he mention some task for which those lacking steel backs or teak knees were disqualified. Then you smiled your defeat.

But in later years Arthur found no use for the smallest subtlety. He made no concession to style or politeness. 'Fancy some tea?' he would begin; then, rising a mere inch from the cushioned funk-hole of his armchair, would utter a lazy 'Ouch' and sink back.

'Shocking, this knee/foot/liver of mine,' he would observe to Marion, and didn't even lay on the over-zealous thanks (which formerly gave him such a kick) when she got up and headed for the kitchen. Other physical defects – some long-standing like recurrent dreams, some the dragonfly fads of an afternoon – prevented him from changing plugs, reaching high shelves, mending his clothes, washing up or seeing us off. One day, when he had confessed to an arthritic thumb, muddy vision and a possibly gangrenous foot within the space of half an hour, Marion suggested a doctor.

'After me money are you? Horse-butchers, all of them. It's in their interests to keep you ill, any fool can see that. So that they can claim more money off the Ministry of Health commissars.'

'But, Arthur,' Marion pretended to protest, 'maybe it's something serious.'

'Nothing that another cushion' (pretending to reach for one) 'can't oooo ooowww thank you lad cure.' Then he added dutifully, 'Blasted knee.'

His meanness, which had previously been subject to coy disguise, gradually assumed the nature of a straightforward pleasure. His dog Ferdinand had died not long after Arthur had decided that there was an unnecessary amount of meat in dog-food. A 50 per cent Pal and 50 per cent wood-shavings mixture had done for Ferdinand. Arthur would have watered its water if he'd known how.

He lost friends as he grew older. He didn't mend his fences, never drew his curtains, and enjoyed annoying his neighbours with prolonged bouts of scratching. The Christmas cards he sent were always recycled, with an ostentatious patch over the previous sender's signature; sometimes, with a sort of gnarled playfulness, he would return to Marion and me the same card we had sent him the Christmas before.

The rest of his correspondence was mainly with the directors of mail-order firms, whom he managed to cheat quite efficiently. His technique was to send off for goods on approval; when they arrived, he would wait a month, despatch a cheque and immediately order his bank not to honour it. When a query arrived from the firm, he wrote back to them at once (but dating the letter two days earlier, so that it would appear to have crossed in the post), complaining of the quality of the goods, demanding a replacement before he sent back the defective item, and asking for advance reimbursement of postal and packing charges. He had other, more Byzantine delaying ploys, and frequently ended up gaining an ex-RNVR officer's heavy-duty parka, or a pair of plastic-handled self-sharpening secateurs, for merely the cost of a few steamed-off stamps and re-used envelopes.

Some of Arthur's infirmities, however, must have been genuine – though I wonder if he himself knew the difference – and ganged together to produce a fatal heart attack. The fact of his death didn't move me much; nor did its lonely circumstances, which were of his own choosing. Instead, what upset me when Nigel and I went to clear up the bungalow was the pathos of objects. While Nigel chattered away about the ghoulish features of dying which interested him, I grew melancholy at the half-finished things which a death persuades you to focus on. The heap of dirty dishes was normal for Arthur, who had once applied for a reduction in his water rate on the grounds that he washed up only every fortnight, and then used the leftover liquid for watering his roses. But everywhere I was impaled by objects that lay freshly abandoned, severed, discarded. A half-empty packet of pipe cleaners with one – the next to be used – projecting from it. Bookmarks (more exactly, scraps of newspaper) sadly noting the point beyond which Arthur would never read (not that I cared, in one sense). Clothes which, though others would have thrown them away, still had five good years of wear in them for Arthur. Clocks which would now run down without any interference. A diary killed off at 23rd June.

The cremation was no worse than a family Christmas, or a changing-room encounter with some rugby team of which you are a reluctant member. Afterwards, we filed out into the hot afternoon, the dozen or so mourners whom Arthur's death had scraped together. We stood around awkwardly, read the wreaths and commented on each other's cars. Some of our wreaths, I noticed, didn't have a sender's name pinned to them; perhaps they had been contributed by the crem to stop us getting depressed at our poor showing.

As Marion drove us home, I held Amy in my arms and

listened to the back-seat prattle of a couple of half-identified relatives. I mused lightly about Arthur's death, about him simply not existing any more; then let my brain idle over my own future non-existence. I hadn't thought about it for years. And then I suddenly realised I was contemplating it almost without fear. I started again, more seriously this time, masochistically trying to spring that familiar trigger for panic and terror. But nothing happened; I felt calm; Amy gurgled happily in reply to the alternating strain and roar of the car. It was like the moment when the Indians go away.

That evening, as Marion sewed and I sat over a book, my conversation with Toni in the garden came back to me. I wondered how far off my death would be: thirty, forty, fifty years? And would I sleep with anyone other than my wife until I died? Screw not, lest thy wife be screwn, Toni had jeered. But that against fifty years? And so far, had I been faithful because I still enjoyed making love to my wife (why that 'still'?)? Is fidelity merely a function of sexual pleasure? If desire slackened, or *timor mortis* rose, what then? And what, in the future, if you suddenly became bored with the same round of friends? Sex, after all, is travel.

'You remember Tim Penny's party?' The time had come, I thought, to disprove some of Toni's assumptions about our marriage.

'Mmmn.' Marion carried on stitching neatly.

'Well, something happened there.' (But why did I feel nervous?)

'Mmmn?'

'I ... met a girl who tried to get off with me.' Marion looked up at me quizzically, then went back to her needle.

'Well, I'm glad I'm not the only person who finds you attractive.'

'No, I mean she tried really quite hard.'

'I can't say I blame her.'

It was odd. Whenever Marion and I start talking about really serious matters I can never predict which way the conversation will go. I don't mean she doesn't understand me;

maybe she understands me too well; but I always feel out-manoeuvred – and I know she isn't manoeuvring.

'I mean, I didn't fancy her back.'

' ... '

'She was quite pretty, actually.'

' ... '

'It just seems to have upset me a bit, that's all.' Shit, I sounded weedy.

'Chris, do be more adult. You just fancied her, that's all.'

'No I didn't – only I suppose I was thinking, well, if we're both about thirty now: it was all in general terms really – I suppose I was wondering if we were going to end up sleeping with other people ever.'

'You mean, you were wondering if you were.' It was like having someone constantly resetting a table you thought you'd laid. 'And the answer is, of course you will,' she said, looking up at me.

'Oh come on ... ' But why did I look away? I felt guilt already, as if she was calmly showing me Polaroids of my humping bum.

'Of course you will. I mean, probably not now, not here; not, I hope to God, ever in this house. But some time. I've never doubted that. Some time. It's too interesting not to.'

'But I haven't tried to, I haven't wanted to.' I felt upset as well as guilty; but also, to be truthful, I didn't want it all previewed; maybe, secretly, I was wanting to save all the emotions – even the unpleasant ones – for later.

'It's all right, Chris. You didn't go into marriage expecting a virgin and I didn't go in expecting a flagrantly faithful husband. Don't think I can't imagine what it's like to be sexually bored.' Oh shit: it was getting out of hand now. I didn't want to hear any of this.

'Honestly, love, I was thinking in very general terms – you know, almost in terms of morality, er,' (feebly) 'philosophy. And I wasn't thinking especially about me. I was thinking about both of us, about ... everyone.'

'You weren't, Chris, otherwise you would have asked about me before now.'

' ... ?'

'And so, even if you aren't asking, you may as well know that the answer is Yes I did once, and Yes it was only once, and No it didn't make any difference to us at the time as we weren't getting on perfectly anyway, and No I don't particularly regret it, and No you haven't met or heard of him.'

Christ. Shit. Fuck. She looked at me, directly, openly, with calm eyes. I was the one who looked away. It was all wrong.

'And I've never been tempted since, and with Amy now I shouldn't think I will be, and it's all right, Chris, it's really all all right.'

Shit. Piss. Fuck. Well, bugger anyway. Well, I suppose that sort of answered my question.

'I suppose that answers my question,' I said ruefully. Marion came across and gently stroked the back of my neck. I liked that.

What was I meant to feel? What did I feel? That it was quite funny really. Also, that it was interesting. Also, that I was half-proud that Marion was still capable of astonishing me. Jealousy, anger, petulance? They would have been a bit out of place. They could hang around for later.

That night I made love to Marion with a hectic diligence. Rather well too, as it turned out. At the end, as she turned over into sleep, Marion surprised me again.

'Was that better?'

'Better than what?'

'That girl at Tim Penny's?' How could she tease me about that when, when ... But then again, I was almost pleased that she could and did.

'Well, she wasn't bad, you know. Really not bad for a young thing. But what I always say is, who wants plonk when you can get château-bottled?'

'Wino,' she chuckled.

'Gourmet,' I corrected her; and we made happy, sleepy noises at each other. Perhaps it really was all all right?

5 · The Honours Board

When I took up Tim Penny's invitation to the old boys' dinner, it was largely in a spirit of satirical curiosity. What were they all like, some twelve, thirteen years after I'd last set eyes on them? Who would be there, whom would I recognise? Would Barton, who sat at the desk in front of me for a whole year when I was fourteen, still have that gristly knob above his left ear; or would it all be camouflaged by blown-dry layer-cutting? Would Steinway still want to dash off to the bog for a quick wank in the middle of things, returning listless but satisfied? Would Gilchrist still be making damp, squelchy noises with his hands (had he gone into the BBC sound effects department?). How many of them would be bald? Had anyone died?

I had a couple of hours to kill before the school served – what? watery fino? – so I arranged to have a drink with Toni. I suggested – since it was only a couple of minutes from Harlow Tewson – that we meet at the National Gallery; but Toni said he didn't visit cemeteries any more. Instead, I dropped in alone for quarter of an hour first.

'Any new gravestones?' Toni enquired with his old squint-grin as we settled over our drinks (white wine for me, whisky and Guinness chaser for him).

'There's a nice Seurat on loan. And that new Rousseau. Though I didn't look at them very closely.' (Toni grunted, gave himself a Guinness moustache) 'I find I always turn left in there: Piero, Crivelli, Bellini, that's what I go for nowadays.'

'Quite right: no point in looking for live stuff in a cemetery. Might as well look at the dead fucks.'

'You have to be dead to get in, don't you?'

'Some are shamming life. But the old fucks who are working within a totally defunct framework – then you can really concentrate on technique and stuff. Crivelli – yeah.'

I didn't like to say that I found Crivelli's saints and martyrs – the drawn, Gothic faces and the 3-D jewels – well, really quite moving.

'Do you remember our silly experiments there?' I was interested to see which way Toni would go.

'What was so sodding silly about them?' I always forgot how quickly he was roused. 'I mean, we were on the right track, weren't we? I admit we were fundamentally misguided in the choice of our specimens: looking for a spark of response in the commuters and hand-jobbers you get going round that place is about as futile as looking for a prong on a eunuch. But at least we were looking, at least we believed that art was to do with something happening, that it wasn't all a water-colour wank.'

'Hmmn.'

'What do you mean, hmmn?'

'Don't you sometimes wonder if that's all it is?'

'Chris ... ' He sounded surprised, disappointed; not angry and contemptuous as I'd half expected. 'Come on, Chris, not you as well. I mean, I know I get at you a lot. But you don't really think that do you?'

For once he seemed capable of being hurt; and I for once felt disinclined to pacify him. I remembered his phrase about Marion and the loofah. 'I don't know. I used to think I knew. I love all of it as much as I ever did: I read, I go to the theatre, I like pictures ... '

'Dead cunts' pictures.'

'Old pictures, OK. I like it all; I always did; I just don't know whether there's any sort of direct link between it and me – whether the connection we force ourselves to believe in is really there.'

'Don't give me Wagner and the Nazis, I beg.'

'OK, but isn't it a bit like the cathedral and religion fallacy? Just because art claims a lot for itself doesn't mean its claims are true.'

'Nooooo,' said Toni, as if to a child.

'And I honestly don't believe our experiments as we called them showed anything much at all.'

'Nooooo.'

'So the only place you can look to find out whether or not it's all a water-colour wank, as you put it, is within yourself.'

'Yeeeah.'

'Well. Well, I suppose that since we started looking I've gradually become less and less convinced.' I glanced up, expecting Toni to be baleful; he was knitting his brows, seeming pained. 'I mean, I don't deny that it's all ... ' I looked up again, nervously ' ... *fun*, and you know, moving and all that stuff as well, and *interesting* too. But in terms of what it actually *does*, what can you say? What can you actually say in favour of the National Gallery?'

'Shit all, I agree.'

'No – agree for the right reasons. Fill it with all the stuff you like, all the stuff which, if you wouldn't lay down your own life for, you might lay a few other people's – and still what have you got? What can you say in its favour except that it keeps people off the streets; that there's a pretty low level of mugging and incest and armed robbery inside the National Gallery?'

'Aren't you being a bit literalist? You sound like some Soviet arts commissar to me – every vork off heart must do somm gut, immediate.'

'No, because that's obviously rubbish too.'

'So what's changed? The art hasn't, boyo. I can tell you that. Looks like a sell-out job to me.'

'That's a pretty silly remark.'

'Well, what's become of you? I mean, even when you were in Paris ... '

'Which is a decade ago. Which is all my adult life ago.'

'Ah – a new definition of "adult": the time during which one has sold out.'

'I told you – in the garden the other week – I just don't see that it makes anything happen. Very nice for us that the Renaissance occurred and all that; but it's all really about ego and aggro, isn't it?'

Toni put on his pedagogue voice again.

'You don't think the effect might be cumulative?'

'I see that it could be; but that doesn't make it any the less theoretical. Either way it seems to depend on an act of faith – and for the moment I've lapsed.'

'Another triumph for the bourgeois steamroller,' Toni noted sadly, almost to himself. 'Travel with your *pantoufles*, do you?'

'You're wrong.'

'Wife, baby, reliable job, mortgage, *flower* garden,' (he stressed it contemptuously) 'can't fool me.'

'What evidence is that? You're not exactly Rimbaud yourself are you?'

'And what are we doing tonight?' Toni was warming up. 'Back off to the old school? Quick visit to some quattrocento dead cunts and then off to the old school? Sounds like a boots-only on the bourgeoisie if you ask me.'

'Well, it's not like that. Sure I'm happy now; who hasn't had that?'

'But the evidence is against you.'

'Then you, from your personal knowledge of me, ought to bloody well know better.'

'Now who's asking for an act of faith?'

The front steps of the school were flanked by a rising row of lamp standards, round which twined iron eels with gaping mouths. Automatically, I glanced up at the high windows of the headmaster's study, from which he had spied gauntly on boys arriving late. Tim and I were formally welcomed in the library by Colonel Barker, ex-head of the CCF, a corpulent man feared for his unpredictability. The area between his second and third waistcoat buttons was spanned by a huge star-shaped medal, slung round his neck on a scarlet ribbon. Was this, I wondered, his famous CBE, once announced to the school in tones more appropriate to foreign conquest? It looked too large and flashy to be British; perhaps he had been given it during the war by some government-in-exile.

'Welcome, Lloyd,' he gruffed at me, and the surname, despite a friendly burr in the voice, brought back old fears of defaulter parades, of rifle grease and wet undergrowth, of having your balls shot off. 'Welcome back to the flock. More pleasure in one that hath strayed, and all that. Ah, Penny, wife well? How are the little halfpennies and farthings? Good. Good.'

The library, scene of so many 'private study periods' (battleships and word games and thumbed copies of *Spick*) was all grey-and-white, the colour of commuters, the colour of businessmen. One or two bricky faces indicated spells abroad with the firm; but mostly they were the worn, indeterminate colour which comes from being surrounded by high buildings, earthed up like asparagus. Over there, wasn't that Bradshaw? And Voss? And that boy who everyone thought was really thick, but still got made a prefect – Gurley? Gowley? Gurney? And – oh Christ – Renton in – oh Christ again – a dog collar; looking just as horribly enthusiastic as ever; nasty little excited eyes implying you ought to be doing something different. From round the room little whoops of recognition rang out, as far-off Corps camps and school plays were recalled.

We trooped downstairs to the dining hall in the basement, where the light pine of my youth had been darkened by time and spilled food; where the honours boards had spread across the walls like creepers; where the long tables reminded me of lunchtimes spent bending cutlery and whizzing salt cellars up and down like drinks in a Western. From backstage came the steamy reek of communal cooking and the clatter of a thousand knives and forks being dropped into a metal bin.

I sat between Penny and Simmons while Colonel Barker from the top table wished us officially welcome again, then bawled '*Bon appétit*' as if he were on the parade ground. Simmons had emerged after all these years looking fairly normal: even his ears seemed to have grown back closer to his head. He turned out to know a lot about railway arcana: dead stations; tunnels people had simply forgotten about, like in Conan Doyle; tales of Blitz nights in the Underground. Penny and I got along well, too, with one of those drinking people-and-places conversations. On the opposite side of the table were faces which, projected back into soft-cheeked spottiness, were recognisable as Lowkes, Leigh, Evans and Pook. News was heard of Gilchrist (in the wine trade), Hilton (a plate-glass academic) and Lennox (back at the school teaching). Thorne had dropped out of sight; Waterfield was in a French jail serving six months for pimping.

At first, my scorn flashed into place automatically: like a batsman, I went on to the back foot for every ball, regardless of length. But as the dinner wore on, I found myself almost enjoying it. Perhaps it's hard, having escaped school and its influences by efforts you yourself deem heroic, to credit others with the same tenacity, the same gritty autonomy. The idea that some of them might have found it an easier, less heroic process than you did is even less acceptable.

'Publishing, I hear?' Leigh (known all those years ago as Ugh) shouted across at me as I launched a geological probe into my trifle in a search for solid bodies. He had a whiny, imprecise voice I'd always disliked; what seemed at first a regional inflection turned out to be only casual articulation.

'More or less; bit of research too, though. Firm called Harlow Tewson.'

'Of course, of course. I've got your gardening book. It's quite good, actually; only trouble is it's so big you need a wheelbarrow to help you get it down the garden.'

I tossed him a heard-it-before smile for the trim suburban quip. The book in question was admittedly bound in imitation weathered teak and was quite heavy; but only a numbskull would consult it anywhere except in the house.

'Yes, yes,' he went on, with a more-of-this-to-come look, 'I left it out one afternoon and suddenly thought, I'd better fetch it in before it sprouts roots and I don't recognise it any more and start staking it. Ha ha. We've got your kitchen book as well.'

This was a thick, square volume, bound in a sort of tin foil, with a portrait of the Queen on the front cover; it was designed to look like a Coronation cake-tin.

'Yes, many's the time I've given it a shake to see if there were any biscuits inside. Ha ha. Why do you think people are always making things nowadays to look like things they aren't? Do you think it's a sort of profound escapism? Do you think the motives are economic or psychological?'

'What do you do?' (I didn't care to follow up that pissy point, thank you very much.)

'Oh, same sort of country, really. I run a little firm called Hidebound Books.'

What, Leigh? I'd somehow assumed the little ... well, nothing specific, though a whole range of unspecified possibilities. So they hadn't all become bank managers as Toni and I had predicted.

'We're only a tiny outfit, but ... '

'Of course – you published Toni's *Muted Manglings*.'

Hidebound Books – the name was planned to contain a double irony – published small neat paperbacks on a variety of subjects; partly gap-filling; partly judicious reprints; but a fair proportion of original stuff. Toni's monograph was in a series called – after Orwell – *As I Please*. In it he argued how all important books are on first publication significantly misunderstood, whether they are praised or panned. If they are panned, there are always those ready for an acrimonious public dispute; but if they are acclaimed, then no one cares about the critics' mistakes. Flaubert said success is always off the mark. It was the farcical bits in *Madame Bovary* that made it a hit. In Toni's view, the psychology of those who acclaim success for the wrong reasons was even more interesting than that of those who decry it for the wrong reasons.

'Yes, we did. It didn't get many notices, but then you

wouldn't expect it to: it was too hot to handle for most of the critical establishment. I quite liked it.'

Leigh then explained to me his principles of business, which seemed to hinge a lot on what he referred to as 'creative bankruptcy'.

'No – really, we're on the up. Setting up a new imprint at the moment. We're going to call it Scavenger Books. Translations of spunkbooks – you know, what other people call seminal works. Mainly French, I should think.'

'Sounds fun.'

'Tempting?'

'How do you mean?'

'We need someone to run it. You've had a good education.' He waved his hand round at the dining-hall (as rowdy now as two decades ago); he smiled what looked to be a non-commercial smile. 'We'll match your salary; travel; get to meet a few *penseurs*.'

'Harlow Tewson aren't going bankrupt to pay my salary.'

'I don't think we will. Look, I've even got a card.' (A fancy piece of Kate Greenaway, with tulips curling tweely round his initials) 'Give me a ring.'

I nodded. The evening began its decline with sweating cheese, coffee and brandy (only fit for tipping in the coffee). Colonel Barker rose, and I suddenly remembered that when we misconjugated verbs he used to twist our ears hard in opposite directions. Yet as he stood there, waiting for his former pupils to quieten down, his medal occasionally dispensing a flash of light from his tub of a belly, he suddenly seemed incapable of ever being frightening again; he had become the sort of person that you might offer your seat to on a train.

'Gentlemen,' he began, 'I was going to say "Boys", but you're all a lot bigger than me now – Gentlemen, whenever I come to these dinners, I always think that things are not half as bad as the newspaper johnnies keep trying to make out. I really do. I've talked to quite a few of you this evening, and without any swollen head stuff I'd like to say I think the School can be jolly well proud of you.' (Banging of cutlery, stamping of feet – it was like the announcement of house colours) 'I know it's fashionable nowadays to disparage anything that's been successful for a number of years, but I'm not going to jump on that boat. I think that if something's been successful for a number of years, then that's because it's GOOD.' (More stamping) 'Still, no politics, no packdrill, so I won't waste your time with what *I* think. I'll just put it this way. When you're as old as I am,' (cries of 'Don't believe it' and 'Shame'; Barker smiled; his voice took on a warm croakiness) 'you'll know how I feel. I've seen a lot of charges pass through my hands: it's like watching a mighty river of boys flowing down to the great sea of adulthood. And we masters are a bit like lock-keepers. We tend the banks; we keep traffic flowing; occasionally' (he looked serious) 'we even have to jump in and pull someone out. And though the water may get choppy at times, we know that this mighty river of boys will get to the sea in the end. Tonight I feel sure that my own modest efforts on your behalf have not gone unrewarded. I'll be able to retire to my lock-keeper's cottage with a sense of pride. I thank you. Now an old man will let you get on with your coffee in peace.'

I got home drunkish (Tim and I had a couple for the rails at the station bar at Baker Street and smirked at Barker's speech) but cheerful. Marion was already in bed, with a huge Bloomsbury biography holding her down like a paperweight. I unlaced my shoes, clambered on to the bed and stuck a hand down the front of her nightdress.

'Forgotten what they're like,' I mumbled.

'Then you must be drunk,' she answered, but not reprovingly.

I took out my hand, pulled the front of her nightdress towards me and breathed heavily down it. I peered in.

'If the tip turns green ... Yes, there we go. You're right again, my love, as always. *I*' (hoisting myself into a kneeling position and gazing at her uxoriously) '*I* have been offered a job this evening by Balldrop Leigh.'

'What as?' She took my hand away from the front of her nightdress, towards which it had been confidently returning. 'What as?'

'Balldrop was called Balldrop,' I went on in the tone of one interviewed in old age, 'because when we went swimming at school, in the nude, as we did until we reached the sixth form, by which I mean that in the sixth form we no longer went swimming at all, but when, previously, we did go, it was always in the nude, and Leigh, I remember, indeed I think anyone of my generation will recall, we can phone Penny if you don't believe me, he'll confirm it, had one ball which hung down, oh, I should say, trick of the memory and all that, but I should say a good two and a half inches below the other. It was the time that elastic-sided boots were becoming fashionable, and we, my friends and I, that is, used to say that Balldrop was the only boy in the world with an elastic-sided scrotum. And now Balldrop is offering me a job. I can't understand it. Haven't I got a job?'

In the course of this speech I managed to insinuate my hand under the bedclothes and work it up under Marion's nightie from the other direction.

'What as?'

But at that point my hand reached a destination of equivalent — if not (who can say?) greater — value to its earlier, thwarted one.

'Stud?' I merely replied, feeling puzzled.

6 · Object Relations

'So this is it?' Toni had said as he stood slyly quizzing my vegetable patch. I hadn't answered; why let someone else cut in on your self-reproaches? You don't need friends for *that*. When I'm chamoising the car in the front drive and some half-familiar face walks past and smiles and raises his stick and points approvingly at a sprinting patch of deckle-edged ivy, don't imagine I can't hear the voice we all give free lodging to in a room at the back of our skulls: the one that goes, fine, all right, fair enough, but someone else – someone who might have been you – is even now sledding through a birch forest in Russia, pursued by wolves. On Saturday afternoons, as I track the lawn mower carefully across our sloping stretch of grass, rev, slow, brake, turn and rev again, making sure to overlap the previous stripe, don't think I can't still quote you Mallarmé.

But what do these complaints urge, except pointless excess and disloyalty to one's character? What do they promise but disorientation and the loss of love? What's so chic about extremes; and why such guilt about the false lure of action? Rimbaud journeyed to Cairo, and what did he write to his mother: '*La vie d'ici m'ennuie et coûte trop.*' As for that sled-and-wolves stuff: there isn't any evidence of a wolf ever killing a man, anywhere. Fancy metaphors can't all be trusted.

I'd call myself a happy man; if preachy, then out of a sense of modest excitement, not pride. I wonder why happiness is despised nowadays: dismissively confused with comfort or complacency, judged an enemy of social – even technological – progress. People often refuse to believe it when they see it; or disregard it as something merely lucky, merely genetic: a few drops of this, a dash of that, a couple of synapses unclogged. Not an achievement.

A noir, E blanc, I rouge ... ? Pay your bills, that's what Auden said.

Last night, Amy woke and began to grizzle quietly. Marion immediately stirred, but I patted her back into sleep.

'I'll see to her.'

I slid out of bed and made for the door which we left propped open so that we could hear Amy. I found my slightly clotted brain praising the constant carpet, the central heating, the double glazing. I was about to feel ashamed of my relief, my pleasure in this material comfort; then I thought, why bother?

By the time I got to Amy's room, she was silent. I was a little alarmed. I fear for her when she cries, and fear for her when she goes quiet. Maybe that's why you find yourself praising the central heating.

But she was breathing normally and lying safely. I mechanically straightened her bedclothes and headed downstairs; I felt fully awake now. I wandered into the sitting-room, emptied an ash-tray, and pushed back the sofa with the pressure of a bare big toe (speaking the advert ironically to myself, 'Ah, those Touchglide castors'). I walked through the hall, glancing at the wire letter-cage on the front door ('Room 101', I always think), and went into the kitchen. The cork tiles are warm to the feet, even warmer than the carpet. I heave myself on to one of our cane bar stools – the sort with a low back rest – and feel lurchingly master of all I survey.

In the road outside is a sodium lamp whose orange light, filtered through a half-grown fir in the front garden, softly lights up the hall, the kitchen, and Amy's bedroom. She enjoys this civic night-light, and prefers going off to sleep with her curtains drawn back. If she wakes, and there is no orange glow pervading her room (the lamp operates on a time-switch, and goes off at two in the morning), she becomes fretful.

I sit on my bar stool in my pyjamas, grip the sink unit, and tip back on to two legs. Then I shift my weight and move on to a single rubber-capped stool-end. I feel a kind of lazy pleasure at being able to do this without overbalancing. I feel a kind of lazy pleasure too at the smooth, clean, dry expanse of stainless steel in front of me. I rotate on the single leg of the stool, holding tight with one hand, then passing the other one behind my back so that I am gripping with both again. Now I am facing in to the room. The table laid for breakfast, the neat line of cups on their hooks, the onions giving off a crepuscular glisten from their hanging basket: everything is orderly, comforting, yet strangely alive. The spoon by my breakfast bowl implies the grapefruit cut and waiting in the refrigerator, the sugar on its surface already hardening into a crust. Objects contain absent people. A poster, flat and pinned, of the château of Combourg (where Chateaubriand grew up) narrates a holiday four years ago. A phalanx of a dozen glasses on a shelf implies ten friends. A feeding-bottle, stored high on a dresser, predicts a second baby. On the floor next to the dresser is a plastic travel-bag with a bright sticker we bought to amuse Amy: 'Lions of Longleat', it says, with a picture of a lion in the middle.

I swing round again, strangely comforted, and face the window. The orange light has turned the stripes in my pyjamas brown. I can't even remember what their original colour is: I have several pairs in different colours, all with the same breadth of stripe, and they all come out a muddy brown in this light. I reflect on this for a few moments, to no particular end. I follow a half-factitious line about the nature of the light: how the sodium with its strength and nearness blots out the effect of even the fullest moon; but how the moon goes on nevertheless; and how this is symbolic of … well, of something, no doubt. But I don't pursue this too seriously: there's no point in trying to thrust false significances on to things.

I stare out of the kitchen window for a few minutes, directly at the street lamp which shines through its gauze of fir. Two o'clock occurs. The lamp snaps off, and I am left with a lozenge-shaped blue-green after-image. I continue to stare; it diminishes, and then, in its turn, and in its quieter way, snaps off.